圖解

Hotel English
Picture Wordbook

旅館英文詞彙

一本餐旅科系學生必備的實用工具書

張雅端　吳玉珍
柳瑜佳　張素蓁

合著

自序

　　這本圖解旅館英文冊子的出版，是規畫中，也是在壓力下。在觀光學院任教的我們，深刻感受到學生在英語學習上的困擾，四年前起念合作編輯適合成績不是那麼好、不是那麼愛讀書、英文基礎不是很好的學生，在專業上需要的英文小冊。規畫針對觀光的幾個面向，餐飲、旅館、旅遊分別編輯在該領域從業人員基本應該要學習的單字或用語小冊子，為了提高學習興趣與成效，以圖解方式幫助記憶，放入筆者在世界各地旅行拍攝的照片，或邀請學生參與拍攝，引發學生的學習興趣與意願。

　　第一本圖解餐飲英文字彙在2010年出版，隔了三年，因為忙，在技職體系院校擔任教職，教學、輔導、行政、研究四者都要接受考核，四者要兼顧，且都要做到很好，非有相當能力者，或犧牲睡眠，難矣！但四人仍決定採取行動，著手進行第二本書。感謝過程中提供協助的所有人，讓這本擱置在電腦硬碟中近一年的小冊子終能出版。

目次

contents

Unit 1

Hotel Staff & Hotel Types

旅館人員及類型

單字特區

Part I: Hotel Types 旅館類型

01 hotel〔ho'tɛl〕
旅館，飯店

02 hostel〔'hastḷ〕
青年旅舍

03 motel〔mo'tɛl〕
汽車旅館

04 resort〔rɪˈzɔrt〕
渡假飯店

05 villa〔ˈvɪlə〕
渡假別墅

06 inn〔ɪn〕
小旅館

07 B & B
（bed and breakfast）
〔bɛd ænd ˈbrɛkfəst〕
（一泊一食）民宿

Part II: Hotel Staff　旅館人員

08 hotel manager
〔hoˈtɛl ˈmænɪdʒɚ〕
飯店經理

09 front desk clerk
〔frʌnt dɛsk klɝk〕
飯店前檯服務人員

10 concierge
〔kɑnsɪ ˈɛrʒ〕
櫃檯服務員

11 bell captain
〔bɛl ˈkæptɪn〕
行李員領班

12 porter〔ˈpɔrtɚ〕
行李員

13 doorman〔ˈdɔrmən〕
門房

14 valet〔ˈvælɪt〕
代客停車員

15 operator〔ˈɑpəretɚ〕
接線生

16 cashier〔kæˈʃɪr〕
出納

17 housekeeper
〔ˈhaus ˈkipɚ〕
房務員

18 laundry staff
〔ˈlɔndrɪ stæf〕
洗衣部人員

19 room division manager
〔rum dəˈvɪʒən ˈmænɪdʒɚ〕
房務部經理

20 fitness center attendant
〔'fɪtnəs 'sɛntɚ ə'tɛndənt〕
健身中心服務員

21 business center attendant
〔'bɪznəs 'sɛntɚ ə'tɛndənt〕
商務中心服務員

22 receptionist
〔rɪ 'sɛpʃənɪst〕
接待員

23 event planner
〔ɪ'vɛnt 'plænɚ〕
活動企劃人員

24 butler〔'bʌtlɚ〕
私人管家

25 maintenance technician
〔'mentənəns tɛk'nɪʃən〕
維修人員

1. hotel：旅館，飯店
   （ex）This five-star hotel features luxurious facilities and
   delicacies.
   這家五星級飯店標榜豪華的設備和精緻的美食。

2. hostel：青年旅舍
   （ex）A hostel is the cheapest of all and thus the best choice
   for the backpackers.
   青年旅舍費用低廉，也因此成為背包客的絕佳選擇。

3. motel：汽車旅館
   （ex）A motel, a hotel designed for motorists, usually has a
   parking area for vehicles.
   汽車旅館，是專門為汽車族設計的旅館，通常都有
   停車場供房客停車。

4. resort：渡假飯店
   （ex）The spa resorts in Hualien focus on helping guests to
   relax and thus attract vacationers all over the world.
   在花蓮以舒緩減壓為號召的溫泉渡假飯店，吸引世
   界各地的觀光客。

5. villa：渡假別墅

（ex）We're going to rent a villa in Yangming Mountain for the coming summer holidays.

這個暑假我們要去陽明山租一棟別墅消暑。

6. inn：小旅館

（ex）We stayed in an old inn on our way to Yorkshire.

到約克郡的路上，我們在一間古老的小旅館過夜。

7. B & B（bed and breakfast）：（一泊一食）民宿

（ex）Many B & Bs in Hualien try to create an aboriginal cultural ambiance.

很多花蓮民宿想要營造一種原住民文化的氣氛。

8. front desk clerk：飯店前檯服務人員

（ex）A front desk clerk is responsible for helping guests to check in to a hotel.

前檯服務人員的工作是協助客人入住。

9. porter：行李員（又可稱bell boy/ bellhop/ bell person/ busboy）

（ex）The porter will take your bags up to your room.

行李員會將您的行李送到客房。

10. concierge：櫃檯服務員

（ex）If you need any information about tour and transportation, you can ask the concierge.

如果你需要任何有關旅遊與交通的資訊，可以詢問大廳櫃檯服務員。

11. housekeeper：房務員（又可稱 room attendant/ maid/ room maid）

（ex）I work in Farglory Hotel as a housekeeper. My job is to make up the rooms and restock supplies.

我在遠雄飯店當房務員，我的主要工作是整房和補充房間用品。

12. butler：私人管家

（ex）Many luxurious hotels offer butler service.

很多豪華飯店都有提供私人管家的服務。

單字補給站

Other Hotel Job Titles   其它旅館人員職稱

1.	general manager	總經理
2.	personnel manager	人事經理
3.	director	協理
4.	lobby duty manager	大廳值班經理
5.	assistant manager	大廳副理
6.	reservationist	訂房員
7.	head housekeeper	房務部主管
8.	room maid	房務員
9.	cleaner	公清人員
10.	restaurant manager	餐飲部經理
11.	executive chef	行政主廚
12.	waiter/ waitress	餐飲服務人員
13.	host/ hostess	帶位員
14.	repair person	維修人員

A Job Interview　求職面試

Manager：Good morning. I'm Jason Lin, the personnel manager. Please take a seat.

Employee：Thank you.

Manager：Could I have your name, please?

Employee：Yes, I'm Jenny Sunders.

Manager：Thank you, Ms. Sunders. Could you tell me something about yourself?

Employee：Well, my name is Jenny, and I'm 19 years old. I'm studying at Taiwan Hospitality and Tourism College and I'll graduate next June.

Manager：Good. Why do you want to work for us?

Employee：You are one of the biggest hotel chains in the world. I think I'd learn a lot and it would be good for my career.

Manager：What do you know about the job duties of a front desk clerk?

Employee：Well, checking guests in and out, things like that...

First Day at Work 第一天工作

Assistant	: Good morning and welcome aboard. I'm the personnel assistant, David. Nice to meet you.
Clerk	: Nice to meet you, David.
Assistant	: Now let me introduce you to your colleagues and help you familiarize with your job.
Clerk	: Thank you.
Assistant	: Peter, this is Jenny, the new front desk clerk.
Bell Captain	: Hello, Jenny. I'm Peter.
Assistant	: Peter is the bell captain who is responsible for handling guests' luggage and showing the guests to their rooms.
Clerk	: Very glad to see you, Peter.
Assistant	: And this is Rosa, the senior worker here. She is the concierge. Her duty is to arrange tours and transportation for guests.
Clerk	: Hello, Rosa! I'm Jenny. Front desk is really challenging work.
Concierge	: You've got that right. You know what exactly you should do?
Clerk	: Well, helping guests check in and out...
Concierge	: Yes, you also need to give information about the hotel, handle guest requests and deal with complaints...

單字考驗區

I. Unscramble the words below.請重組下列單字。

1. etavl _____   5. chirsae _____

2. oprarote _____   6. erbtul _____

3. rproet _____   7. amanerg _____

4. swreasit _____   8. oodrnam _____

II. Match each job title with its description.

請將下列職稱與其工作職責配對。

1. _____ waiter/ waitress

2. _____ valet

3. _____ bell captain

4. _____ front desk clerk

5. _____ housekeeper

6. _____ cashier

7. _____ maintenance technician

A. handling the payments

B. helping guests check in and out

C. taking guests' orders in the restaurant

D. parking cars for guests

E. maintaining and repairing the facilities

F. carrying luggage for guests

G. cleaning rooms and restocking supplies

III. Complete the conversations with the words given in the box.

請完成下列對話。

front desk clerk	valet	housekeeper	porter

1. A：What do you do for a living?

　B：I am a _____

　A：What are your duties?

　B：I am responsible for cleaning guests' rooms.

2. A：Where do you work?

　B：I work at Promiseland Hotel.

　A：Oh, really. What do you do there?

　B：I am a _____ . I park cars for hotel guests.

3. A：What do you do here?

　B：I am a _____ .

　A：What are you duties?

　B：I show guests to their rooms and carry their baggage.

4. A：What hotel do you work at?

　B：I work at Hilton Hotel.

　A：What exactly do you do there?

　B：I am responsible for helping guests check in and out.

　　I am a _____ .

　　旅館類型（hotel types）的區分是依據規模、功能目的、費用等，做不同性質的區分。世界各地並無統一的區分標準及類型，甚至稱呼也不同。經濟合作暨發展組織（The Organization for Economic Cooperation and Development, OECD）將住宿的類型分為11種，包括Hotels、Motels、Inns、B&B、Parados、Timeshare、Resort、Condominiums、Camps、Youth Hostels和Health Spas。美國汽車協會AAA（American Automobile Association）的分類為，Hotel（觀光飯店）、Inn（一般旅館）、Motel（汽車旅館）、Country Hotel（鄉村旅館）、Historical Hotel（古蹟旅館）、Lodge（度假小屋）、Cottage（度假農牧場）、Ranch（農牧場）、Apartment（出租公寓）、Suites（出租套房）、Resort（度假旅館）。

　　維基百科（Wikipedia）介紹hotel types中有一類是獨特性旅館（Unique hotels），包括Treehouse hotels、Straw bale hotels、Bunker hotels、Cave hotels、Cliff hotels、Capsule hotels、Ice, snow and igloo hotels、Garden hotels、Underwater hotels、Railway hotels。這些旅館都是具有特色且獨特性的，

如在土耳其中部Cappadocia Goreme的洞穴旅館（cave hotels），是當地穴居文化遺留下來改建的，這些在岩壁鑿洞的「建築」，當年是因為躲避異教徒追趕，善用當地奇岩地形，形成具有特色的穴居文化。Kelebek Pension是其中頗負盛名的洞穴旅館，在觀光旺季往往得幾個月前就預訂呢！旅館裡的房間因為地形關係，每間大小、格局都不同，雖然沒有現代化五星級飯店的豪華設備，但溫馨又具有特色，而且可以體驗當地的文化。

Notes

Notes

Unit 2

Taking Reservations

2007　7 22

訂房

Ocean Cloud Hotel Reservation Form

Ocean Cloud Hotel:		
Please check the room types that you wish to reserve. Room rates are inclusive of all taxes. Breakfasts are included.		
Room with ocean view	☐ Single Room $6,000	☐ Double Room $10,000
	☐ Twin Room $12,000	☐ Family Room $18,000
Room with a balcony	☐ Single Room $8,000	☐ Double Room $12,000
	☐ Twin Room $14,000	☐ Family Room $19,000
Room with mountain view	☐ Single Room $4,000	☐ Double Room $6,000
	☐ Twin Room $8,000	☐ Family Room $10,000
Total amount		

Guest Details:			
Guest Name:			
Family Name:		First Name:	
Address:			
Zip Code/ Postal Code:		City/ Town:	
County/ Province/ State:		Country:	
Contact Number:		Fax:	
Contact e-mail:			
No. of guests/ occupants:		_____ Adults _____ Children	
Check in date:		Check out date:	
No. of nights (length of stay):		_____ nights	
Special requests (subject to availability): ☐ Extra bed ☐ Baby cot (tick if required)			
Smoking preference: ☐ No preference ☐ Smoking ☐ Non-smoking			

Payment:

Accommodation will not be confirmed unless one of the payment methods listed below is used to guarantee your reservation. Reservation is valid upon the confirmation of the hotel.

Name on card:

Credit Card type	☐ Visa	☐ American Express
	☐ Master Card	☐ Others

Credit Card Number:	Expiration Date:
Total amount:	
Deposit	

20% of the total amount as a deposit is required upon booking.

Special requests:

Choose below if there are any specific requirements from the hotel. Requests cannot be guaranteed and are subject to availability upon arrival.

☐ Please note early arrival.

☐ Please note late arrival. (after 7 pm)

☐ Please note late check out.

☐ If possible, please provide adjoining rooms.

☐ Please provide inter-connecting rooms.

☐ Please note passengers are honeymooners.

☐ Please note previous night is booked for early morning arrival.

☐ Please note late arrival at ____ hours ____ minutes (24hr)

☐ Please note early arrival at ____ hours ____ minutes (24hr)

Cancellation Policy:

- No fees if cancellation occurs more than 21 days prior to arrival.

- Cancellation fee of US$20 if you cancel after the confirmation voucher has been issued.

- There is a fee equivalent to the cost of one night's accommodation for all bookings cancelled up to 7 working days prior to the check-in date.

- All bookings cancelled within 3 days prior to the check-in date will incur a 100% charge.

- Cancellation on the same day or no-shows for a reservation will result in a 100% charge. On no account will any monies be refunded.

- All amendments are subject to availability. Some surcharges will be incurred if you do not adhere to the amendment policy of the hotel.

Should you need any further assistance, please do not hesitate to contact us.

Date: ─────────────────────────   Signature:─────────────────────────

Ocean Cloud Hotel Reservation Form

Ocean Cloud Hotel		
Please check the room types that you wish to reserve. Room rates are inclusive of all taxes.		
Room Type 03	Room Rate 04	
Room with ocean view	☐ Single Room $6,000	☐ Double Room $10,000
	☐ Twin Room $12,000	☐ Family Room $18,000
Room with a balcony	☐ Single Room $8,000	☐ Double Room $12,000
	☐ Twin Room $14,000	☐ Family Room $19,000
Room with mountain view	☐ Single Room $4,000	☐ Double Room $6,000
	☐ Twin Room $8,000	☐ Family Room $10,000
Total amount		

* Breakfast included. 05

01 make a reservation〔mek ə ˌrɛzɚˈveʃən〕訂房

02 on-line booking〔ˈɑnˌlaɪn ˈbʊkɪŋ〕線上訂房

03 room type〔rum taɪp〕房型

04 room rate〔rum ret〕房價

05 breakfast included〔ˈbrɛkfəst ɪnˈkludɪd〕含早餐

Guest Details (1) :	
Check in 06 date : 07	Check out 08 date :
No. of guests/occupants : 09	__ Adults 10 __Children 11
No. of nights（length of stay）:	_____ nights
Smoking preference : ☐ No preference ☐ Smoking 12 ☐ Non-smoking 13	
Special requests（subject to availability）: ☐ 14 Extra bed ☐ Baby cot（tick if required）	

06 check in〔tʃɛk ɪn〕住房

07 date〔det〕日期

08 check out〔tʃɛk aʊt〕退房

09 guest〔gɛst〕/ occupant〔'akjəpənt〕房客

10 adult〔ə'dʌlt〕成人

11 children〔'tʃɪldrən〕孩童

12 smoking〔'smokɪŋ〕吸煙的

13 non-smoking〔ˌnan 'smokɪŋ〕非吸煙的

14 extra bed〔'ɛkstrə bɛd〕加床

Guest Details (2)：			
Guest name 15			
Last Name：16			
First Name：17			
Address：18			
Zip code：19		City/Town：20	
County/21 Province/State：		Country：22	
Contact Number：23		Fax：	
Contact e-mail：			

15 guest name〔gɛst nem〕房客姓名

16 last name〔læst nem〕姓

17 first name〔fɝst nem〕名

18 address〔ə'drɛs〕地址

19 zip code〔'zɪp kod〕郵遞區號

20 city〔'sɪtɪ〕/ town〔taʊn〕城市

21 county〔'kʌntɪ〕郡/ province〔'prɑvɪns〕省
state〔stet〕州

22 country〔'kʌntrɪ〕國家

23 contact number〔'kɑntækt 'nʌmbɚ〕連絡電話

Payment：		
Accommodation will not be confirmed unless one of the payment methods listed below is used to guarantee your reservation. Reservation is valid upon the confirmation of the hotel.		
Name on card：		
Card type	☐ Visa	☐ American Express
	☐ Master Card	☐ Others
Credit Card Number：㉔		Expiration Date：㉕
Total amount：		
Deposit：㉖		

*Breakfast included.

*20% of the total amount as a deposit is required upon booking.

㉔ credit card number〔'krɛdɪt kard 'nʌmbɚ〕信用卡號

㉕ expiration date〔ˌɛkspə'reʃən det〕有效期限

㉖ deposit〔dɪ'pazɪt〕訂金

Special Requests：27

Choose below if there are any specific requirements from the hotel. Requests cannot be guaranteed and are subject to availability upon arrival.

☐ Please note early arrival.

☐ Please note late arrival.（after 7 pm）

☐ Please note late check out.

☐ If possible, please provide adjoining rooms.

☐ Please provide inter-connecting rooms.

☐ Please note passengers are honeymooners.

☐ Please note previous night is booked for early morning arrival.

☐ Please note late arrival at _____ hours _____ minutes（**24hr**）

☐ Please note early arrival at _____ hours _____ minutes（**24hr**）

27 special requests〔'spɛʃəl rɪ'kwɛsts〕

額外要求

special requests額外要求：

也可能是使用additional requests、specific requirements或是 special requirements。

Cancellation Policy： 28

• No <u>fees</u> 29 if cancellation occurs more than 21 days prior to arrival.
• Cancellation fee of US$20 if you cancel after the confirmation voucher has been issued.
• There is a fee equivalent to the cost of one night's <u>accommodation</u> 30 for all bookings cancelled up to 7 working days prior to the check-in date.
• All bookings cancelled within 3 days prior to the check-in date will incur a 100% charge.
• Cancellation on the same day or <u>no-shows</u> 31 for a reservation will result in a 100% charge. On no account will any monies be refunded.
• All <u>amendments</u> 32 are subject to availability. Some <u>surcharges</u> 33 will be incurred if you do not adhere to the amendment policy of the hotel.

28 cancellation policy〔ˌkænsəˈleʃən ˈpaləsɪ〕退訂規則

29 fee〔fi〕費用

30 accommodation〔əˌkaməˈdeʃən〕住宿

31 no-show〔no ʃo〕未出現

32 amendment〔əˈmɛndmənt〕修改訂房

33 surcharge〔ˈsɝˌtʃardʒ〕額外費用

實用例句

1. make a reservation：訂房

    （ex）Good morning. I'd like to make a reservation for a double room for three nights.

    早安，我想要訂一間雙人房，訂三個晚上。

2. on-line booking：線上訂房

    （ex）I have made a reservation through on-line booking system.

    我已經透過線上訂房系統訂好房間了。

3. breakfast included：含早餐

    （ex）Is breakfast included in the room rate?

    房價已包含早餐了嗎？

4. guest：房客

    （ex）There are four guests in Room 701, including two adults and two children.

    701房有4位客人，包括2位大人及2個小孩。

5. contact number：連絡電話

    （ex）May I have your contact number, please?

    請問您的連絡電話？

6. credit card number：信用卡號
   （ex）Would you please tell me your credit card number?
   請問您的信用卡號碼？

7. expiration date：有效期限
   （ex）What's the expiration date of your credit card?
   請問您的信用卡有效期限？

8. check-out date：退房日期
   （ex）What's the check-out date? How long are you staying in our hotel?
   請問您的退房日期？預計要在我們旅館住幾天？

9. special requests：額外要求
   （ex）Should you have any special requests, please do not hesitate to contact us.
   如需任何其他服務，歡迎與我們聯繫。

10. deposit：訂金
    （ex）20% of the total amount as a deposit is required upon booking.
    於訂房時需支付總金額的20％作為訂金。

I. Other vocabulary from the reservation form.
訂房表內其他字彙

1. make a reservation   訂房
   = make a booking
   = reserve a room
   = book a room

2. last name   姓氏
   = surname
   = family name

3. first name   名字
   = given name

4. zip code   郵遞區號
   = postal code

5. expiration date   有效期限
   = validity date
   = expiry date

6. deposit   訂金
   = advance payment

7. amendment   修改訂房
   = changes

8. view   景觀

9. balcony   陽台

10. inclusive of tax   含稅

11. amount	總數、總額
12. preference	偏愛
13. fax	傳真
14. baby cot	兒童搖床
15. detail	詳情、細節
16. payment	付款
17. guarantee	保證、擔保
18. early arrival	早到
19. late arrival	晚到
20. late check-out	延後退房
21. adjoining room	相鄰的房間
22. inter-connecting room	內部相通的房間
23. honeymooner	度蜜月的人
24. prior to	在...以前
25. confirmation voucher	確認函
26. issue	核發
27. equivalent	等值的
28. incur	造成、帶來
29. charge	收費
30. on no account	決不
31. refund	退費
32. subject to	視…而定
33. availability	可得性
34. adhere to	遵守
35. amendment	修正、修改
36. complimentary buffet breakfast	免費提供中西式自助早餐

II. English-Chinese version of the reservation form.

訂房表中英對照。

Ocean Cloud Hotel Reservation Form
海雲飯店訂房表

Ocean Cloud Hotels		
Please check the room types that you wish to reserve. Room rates are inclusive of all taxes. 請查看您想預訂的房間類型。所有房價均含稅。		
Room Type 房型	Room Rate 房價	
Room with ocean view 海景房	☐ Single Room $6,000 單人房	☐ Double Room $10,000 雙人房
	☐ Twin Room $12,000 雙床房	☐ Family Room $18,000 家庭/四人房
Room with a balcony 陽台房	☐ Single Room $8,000 單人房	☐ Double Room $12,000 雙人房
	☐ Twin Room $14,000 雙床房	☐ Family Room $19,000 家庭/四人房
Room with mountain view 山景房	☐ Single Room $4,000 單人房	☐ Double Room $6,000 雙人房
	☐ Twin Room $8,000 雙床房	☐ Family Room $10,000 家庭/四人房
Total amount 總額		

* Breakfast included. 含早餐

Guest Details (1)： 房客資訊	
Check in date：住房日期	Check out date：退房日期
No. of guests/occupants： 房客人數	__ Adults __Children __ 成人 __小孩
No. of nights（length of stay）： 停留期間	_____ nights _____ 個晚上
Smoking preference：吸菸與否 ☐ No preference　均可 ☐ Smoking 吸菸 ☐ Non-smoking 不吸菸	
Special requests（subject to availability）： 其他要求（視飯店能否提供） ☐ Extra bed　加床 ☐ Baby cot（tick if required）嬰兒床	

Guest Details (2)： 房客資訊			
Guest name　房客姓名			
Last Name：姓			
First Name：名			
Address： 地址			
Zip code： 郵遞區號		City/Town： 城市	
County/ 　Province/State： 郡/省/州		Country： 國家	
Contact Number： 連絡電話		Fax： 傳真	
Contact e-mail： 電子郵件信箱			

Payment： 付費		
Accommodation will not be confirmed unless one of the payment methods listed below is used to guarantee your reservation. Reservation is valid upon the confirmation of the hotel. 若是您未能以下列的付款方式之一付費，您的訂房將無法確認。所有訂房必須依飯店確認為準。		
Name on card： 持卡人姓名		
Card type 信用卡類別	☐ Visa Visa卡	☐ American Express 美國運通卡
	☐ Master Card 萬事達卡	☐ Others 其他
Credit Card Number： 信用卡號碼	Expiration Date： 信用卡到期日	
Total amount： 總額		
Deposit： 訂金		

*Breakfast included.

*含早餐。

*20% of the total amount as a deposit is required upon booking.

*於訂房時需支付總金額的20％作為訂金。

Special Requests： 額外要求
Choose below if there are any specific requirements from the hotel. Request cannot be guaranteed and are subject to availability upon arrival. 如果您有任何其他特殊要求，請從下面飯店選項中選擇。您的特殊要求要視抵達時飯店實際情況而定。
☐ Please note early arrival. 　請註明會早到。
☐ Please note late arrival.（after 7 pm） 　請註明會晚到。（晚上7點以後）
☐ Please note late check out. 　請註明要延後退房。
☐ If possible, please provide adjoining rooms. 　如果可能，請提供相鄰的房間。
☐ Please provide inter-connecting rooms. 　請提供內部連通的房間。
☐ Please note passengers are honeymooners. 　請註明房客是度蜜月。
☐ Please note previous night is booked for early morning arrival. 　請註明前一天晚上於清晨抵達。
☐ Please note late arrival at ____ hours _____ minutes（**24hr**） 　請註明會延後抵達，在___小時___分鐘（**24小時制**）
☐ Please note early arrival at ____ hours _____ minutes（**24hr**） 　請註明會提前抵達，在___小時___分鐘（**24小時制**）

Cancellation Policy： 退訂規則
• No fees if cancellation occurs more than 21 days prior to arrival. 如果在抵達前21天取消，不收取任何取消的費用。
• Cancellation fee of US$20 if you cancel after the confirmation voucher has been issued. 如果您在確認券已經發出後才取消，費用為20美元。
• There is a fee equivalent to the cost of one night's accommodation for all bookings cancelled up to 7 working days prior to the check-in date. 預訂入住日期前7個工作日內取消，將收取相當於一晚的住宿費。
• All bookings cancelled within 3 days prior to the check-in date will incur a 100% charge. 預訂入住日期前3天內取消將收取100%的費用。
• Cancellation on the same day or no-shows for a reservation will result in a 100% charge. On no account will any money be refunded. 預訂住房當日取消或當天未出現，將收取100%的費用。在任何情形下都不退還已預付之費用。
• All amendments are subject to availability. Some surcharges will be incurred if you do not adhere to the amendment policy of the hotel. 所有修改都視情況而定。如果您未能遵守飯店的修改政策，將產生一些額外費用。

Making a reservation　飯店訂房

Clerk：Ocean Cloud Hotel. Good morning. Can I help you?

Guest：Hello. Do you have any twin rooms available for next Friday and Saturday nights?

Clerk：Just a moment. I'm sorry. There's no twin room left. But we still have double rooms. Would that be OK?

Guest：How much is a double room on weekends?

Clerk：It's NT$3,500.

Guest：OK, then I'd like to reserve a double room.

Clerk：Certainly, madam. When will you be arriving?

Guest：We'll be arriving at about 6:00 p.m. on May seventh.

Clerk：May I have your name, please?

Guest：Yes. It's Nora Adams.

Clerk：May I have your credit card number, Ms. Adams?

Guest：It's 4563 1235 2259 7890.

Clerk：Could you tell me the expiration date?

Guest：It's December 2015.

Clerk：Could you give me a contact number?

Guest：Sure. It's (02) 8669-1744.

Clerk：The room is reserved under your name. Thank you for calling, Ms. Adams. We'll be looking forward to seeing you on May seventh.

單字考驗區

I. Fill in the following ordinal numbers. 填寫下列序數。

MON.	TUE.	WED.	THU.	FRI.	SAT.	SUN.
		1 first	2 second	3 third	4 fourth	5 fifth
6	7	8	9	10	11	12
13	14	15	16	17	18	19
20	21	22	23	24	25	26
27	28	29	30	31		

II. Reorganize the words below. 生字字母順序重組。

1. iiepxraont _____

2. eugst _____

3. tdpeosi _____

4. rneteovsair _____

5. eicrdt arcd _____

6. kobigon _____

7. drdesas _____

8. cckhe otu _____

III. Use the model conversation on the previous page to complete the reservation form.根據前一頁的對話完成下表。

Student A：Ask Student B questions to fill out the form below.

The Ocean Cloud Hotel Reservation Form			
Guest Name：			
Address：			
Phone：			
Room Type：	☐ Single	☐ Double	☐ Family
Date of Arrival：			
Date of Departure：			
Credit Card Number：			
Expiration Date：			

Student B：Reserve a hotel room with the information below.

Larry Robertson
1336 University Boulevard, Taipei, R.O.C.
Phone Number： (886) 2 332-1780
Room：Double room
Arrive：June 10th
Stay：3 nights
Credit Card Number：4563 3345 2578 9901
Expiration Date：12/19

　　自助旅行，如果不想到當地再提著行李找住宿，就必須事先安排好。尤其是在觀光旺季，或者有特定想住的旅館，提前預訂住宿是必要的。預訂住宿除了透過旅行社代訂，網路訂房中心也可以提供服務。

　　幾個好用又可信任的國際訂房中心如，HotelClub、Octopustravel、Agoda。這幾個訂房網有多種語言（包括繁體中文），可以選擇付款貨幣，可以依國家、地區、星級、區域、飯店名稱來做查詢。網站中對飯店的介紹包括設施、客房資訊、位置、照片、旅客評論，甚至互動式地圖等，可以對該飯店有大概的掌握，針對需求做選擇。善用這些訂房中心，貨比三家，有時可以撿到很便宜的優惠價格。

　　這些網路訂房中心提供了多元選擇及便利性，一般的飯店（hotel）多半可透過這些訂房中心預訂，但民宿或一些具歷史性、獨特性的旅館，往往就沒有提供，而要以email、傳真或旅館民宿自己的網站，直接向該旅館或民宿預訂。透過這些網站訂房時要留意上面的條件，如，價格是否含早餐、是否含稅；在做訂房動作最後確認前，一定要看清楚上面的條款，如，是否允許變更或取消，變更或取消的費用；如

有其它需求，也要一併註明，如提早入住、較晚抵達等。

　　一般飯店的房價會依淡旺季、平日及週末而有所分別，旺季及週末的價格較高。有些國家或飯店，還有所謂早鳥（early bird）優惠，愈早訂房價格愈低，德國的飯店多半如此。

相關國際訂房中心網址：
HotelClub
http://www.hotelclub.com/

Octopustravel
http://www.octopustravel.com/

Agoda
http://www.agoda.com.tw/

Notes

Unit 3

Checking in

入住

單字特區

01 check-in counter
〔tʃɛk ɪn 'kaʊntɚ〕
入住櫃檯

02 vacancy〔'vekənsɪ〕
空房

Special Requests

Choose below if there are any specific requirements from the property. Request cannot be guaranteed and are subject to availability on arrival

☐ If possible please provide non-smoking rooms
☐ Please note early arrival **3**
☐ Please note late arrival (after 7 pm) **4**
☐ Please note late check out **5**
☐ If possible, please provide adjoining rooms
☐ Please provide inter-connecting rooms
☐ Please note passengers are honeymooners
☐ Please note previous night is booked for early morning arrival.
☐ Please note late arrival at ⌄ Hours ⌄ Minutes (24hr 🕐)
☐ Please note early arrival at ⌄ Hours ⌄ Minutes (24hr 🕐)

03 early arrival〔ɝlɪ ə'raɪvl̩〕(early check-in)提前入住

04 late arrival〔let ə'raɪvl̩〕(late check-in)延後入住

05 late check-out〔let 'tʃɛk aʊt〕延後退房

Ocean·Cloud·Hotel·Registration·Form

Please present the confirmation voucher and fill up this form upon check-in.

☐ Mr.	☐ Ms.	☐ Mrs.

Personal Information:

Family Name:		First Name:	
Complete Address:			
City:	Country:		Nationality:
Telephone:		Fax:	
E-mail:			
Company/Organization:			
Profession:			
Arrival Date:		Departure Date:	

Payment Information:

Accommodation will not be confirmed unless one of the payment methods listed below is used to guarantee your reservation.

☐ Visa	☐ Master Card	☐ American Express	☐ Bank Transfer
Credit Card Number:		Expiration Date:	
Card Holder's Name:			

Ocean·Cloud·Hotel:

Please check the hotel that you wish to reserve:

Room with ocean view	☐ Single Room	☐ Double Room
Room with a balcony	☐ Single Room	☐ Double Room

Cancellation Policy:

● No fees if cancellation occurs more than 21 days prior to arrival.

● Cancellation on the same day or no-shows will be charged on full night.

Date: --------------------------------- Signature:---

06 registration form 〔ˌrɛdʒɪ'streʃən fɔrm〕住房登記表

To: Chang
From: HotelClub - Aust Business No: 85 092 445 442
Website URL: www.hotelclub.com

──────────── CONFIRMATION VOUCHER ────────────

Booking ID: 41070807
In/Out: In: 22-Jul-2010, Out: 23-Jul-2010, Nights: 1
Guest Name: Chang
Hotel: Queens Hotel Kandy
Hotel Address: Dalada Veediya
Kandy
Hotel Phone: 94-11-4741650

Rooms / Adults and Children

Room		Number	Room		Adults	Children
Standard Room	Twin	1	Standard Room	Twin	2	
			Total		2	

Other Services and Free Benefits

Service		Number	Date
Inclusions	Breakfast	1	Each Day Of Stay

PLEASE NOTE:

1. You must present this confirmation voucher together with photo ID to the hotel receptionist upon check in.

2. If you have any questions regarding your booking, or you require to amend/cancel the booking, you must contact HotelClub (Aust Business No: 85 092 445 442) by phone, fax or e-mail:

Phone: +61 2 8263 5111 or +61 2 8263 5137
Fax: +61 2 9264 0429
E-mail: Chinese@hotelclub.com

3. Please Note Amendments/Cancellations will incur fees as per the booking conditions accepted.
- Cancellation fee of USD 15 if you cancel after the confirmation voucher has been issued.
- 1 night(s) accommodation cost if you cancel 4 day(s) prior to checkin date or later, or if you failed to arrive at your hotel. The cancellation fee of USD 15 will NOT be charged in this case.

4. For any room facilities, hotel facilities and car parking enquiries, please contact the hotel directly on 94-11-4741650.

5. This voucher is to be signed by the registered guest checking into the hotel and must be presented to the hotel on check-in:

I, **Chang**, hereby declare that I am the registered guest for this reservation.

Signature: _____   Date: _____

IMPORTANT NOTE TO HOTEL

Invoice for the above services will be settled by **HOTELCLUB - AUST BUSINESS NO: 85 092 445 442. Under no circumstances must you charge the guest for the services listed on this voucher.** Any additional charges are to be billed direct to the guest and collected by the hotel at the time of service. **Please ensure the voucher is signed when presented by the guest and retained together with your registration form for future reference.** Please send your invoice and a copy of the customer's signed confirmation voucher by email to orbitzforhotels-EMEAandAPAO@orbitz.com. Please quote the following reference on the invoice: **41070807 CHANG 100722.**

 confirmation voucher〔ˌkɑnfə˞ˈmeʃən ˈvaʊtʃə˞〕確認函

08 credit card voucher
〔'krɛdɪt kard 'vaʊtʃɚ〕
信用卡簽單

09 credit card guarantee
〔'krɛdɪt kard ˌgærən'ti〕
信用卡訂房擔保

10 ID（identification）
〔aɪˌdɛntəfə'keʃən〕
證件

11 passport〔'pæsˌpɔrt〕
護照

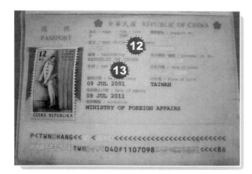

12 nationality
〔ˌnæʃəˈnælətɪ〕
國籍

13 gender
〔ˈdʒɛndɚ〕
性別

14 arrival date
〔əˈraɪvl det〕
入住日期

15 departure date
〔ˌdɪˈpartʃɚ det〕
退房日期

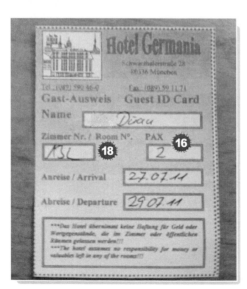

16 No. of nights
〔ˈnʌmbɚ əv naɪts〕
停留時間

17 signature
〔ˈsɪɡˌnətʃɚ〕
簽名

18 room number
〔rum ˈnʌmbɚ〕
房號

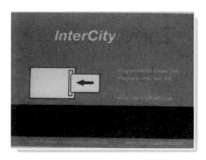 

19 room card〔rum kɑrd〕房卡
room key〔rum ki〕房間鑰匙

20 breakfast voucher〔'brɛkfəst 'vautʃɚ〕早餐券

21 baggage〔'bægɪdʒ〕/
luggage〔'lʌgɪdʒ〕
行李

22 baggage deposit
〔'bægɪdʒ dɪ'pɑzɪt〕
行李暫存

實用例句

1. vacancy：空房

（ex）Guest：Excuse me. Do you have any vacancy for tonight?

Clerk：Yes, we do. There is a single room available.

顧客：請問今晚還有空房嗎？

櫃檯：我們有一間單人房的空房。

2. registration form：住房登記表

（ex）Guest：Ms. Chen. Would you please fill out this registration form?

Clerk：Yes, of course.

櫃檯：陳小姐，可以麻煩您填寫住房登記表？

顧客：好的。

3. ID（identification）：證件

（ex）Clerk：May I see your ID, please?

Guest：Sure, no problem. Here is my passport.

櫃檯：我可以看一下您的證件嗎？

顧客：當然沒問題。這是我的護照。

4. room number：房號

（ex）Clerk：Ms. Chen. The room number is 607. It's on the sixth floor. Here's your room key.

Guest：Thank you.

櫃檯：您的房間在6樓的607。這是您的房門鑰匙。

顧客：謝謝。

5. breakfast voucher：早餐券

  （ex）Guest：Excuse me. You just gave me the breakfast vouchers for tomorrow morning. But we are staying for two nights.

     Clerk：I'm sorry, ma'am. I will give you the other two right away.

     顧客：請問一下，你只給我們明天的早餐券，可是我們住兩個晚上。

     櫃檯：抱歉，女士，我馬上補給您。

6. late check-out：延後退房

  （ex）Guest：Excuse me. Can we have a late check-out until 14:00 tomorrow?

     Clerk：Yes, that will be no problem. I'll keep a record of your special request.

     顧客：請問我們明天可以延後退房嗎？

     櫃檯：沒問題，我會記下您的特殊需求。

7. baggage：行李

  （ex）Clerk：Do you have any baggage?

     Guest：Yes, two pieces.

     Clerk：The porter will help you with the baggage in a minute.

     Guest：Thank you very much.

     櫃檯：您有行李嗎？

     顧客：有的，有兩件。

     櫃檯：行李員馬上會幫您提行李。

     顧客：多謝。

單字補給站

1. check-in counter入住櫃檯，又稱為front desk。

2. credit card guarantee信用卡擔保：在辦理住房時，飯店可能會要求客人提供信用卡擔保，擔保在住宿期間客房服務的可能花費。有些飯店則會註明，請房客提供信用卡資料方可完成保證訂房，但信用卡僅使用於保證訂房，不作他用。

3. No. of nights停留時間，有時會以length of stay呈現。

4. credit card voucher信用卡簽單，也稱為credit card slip.

Conversation A. Larry Chen is at the check-in counter. 辦理飯店住房

Clerk：Good afternoon, sir. How may I help you?

Guest：I'd like to check in, please.

Clerk：Certainly, sir. Do you have a reservation?

Guest：Yes, I do.

Clerk：May I have your name, please?

Guest：Larry Chen.

Clerk：One moment, please. Yes, Mr. Chen. A double room for three nights, starting May 5th.

Guest：Yes, that's right.

Clerk：Would you please fill out this registration form for us?

Guest：Yes, of course.

Clerk：Thank you, sir. May I see your passport, please?

Guest：There you go.

Clerk：Thank you, sir. How are you going to pay, sir?

Guest：By credit card.

Clerk：The hotel policy requires the guest to provide a credit card guarantee.

Guest：Yes, I understand. Here is my visa card.

Clerk：Thank you sir. And this is the credit card voucher for three nights. Please make sure the amount is correct and then sign here. And this is the credit card guarantee. We will confirm the amount with you on the day you check out.

Guest：That's OK.

Clerk：Here is your credit card back. And this is the room card and these are the breakfast vouchers. Your room number is 607 on the 6th floor. Breakfast is served in the main restaurant on the first floor from 6:30 to 10:00 a.m. daily.

Guest：Thank you very much.

Clerk：The porter will help you with your baggage in a minute. Do you need anything else, sir?

Guest：No, that'll be all. Thanks.

Clerk：Thank you, sir. Enjoy your stay with us.

Conversation B. A guest without a reservation is at the front desk.　無事先訂房

Clerk：Good evening, sir. May I help you?

Guest：Good evening. Do you have any vacancy for tonight?

Clerk：One moment, please. I'm sorry, sir. But we are fully booked today.

Guest：Oh, no. What should I do? I need a place to stay.

Clerk：Shall we check the other hotels for you?

Guest：Yes, please. That would be nice. Thank you.

Clerk：Just a moment, please.

I. Write down the Chinese for the following vocabulary.

寫出下列生字對應之中文

Ocean Cloud Hotel Registration Form					
Please present the confirmation voucher and fill up this form upon check-in.					
☐ Mr.		☐ Ms.		☐ Mrs.	
Family Name(1)		First Name(2)			
Complete Address： 10411, No. 5, Lane 7, Section 2, University Road, Taipei, Taiwan, R.O.C.					
City(3)		State(4)		Country(5)	
Zip code(6)		Nationality(7)			
Telephone：886-2-82231234		Fax：886-2-82234321			
E-mail：	larrychen@bim.com.tw				
Company/Organization：	BIM Electronics Ltd.				
Profession：	Engineer				
Arrival Date(8)		Departure Date(9)			
No. of nights(10)		Flight Carrier		CA 888	
Credit Card Type(11)	☐ Visa ☐ Master Card ☐ American Express				
Credit Card Number(12)		Expiration Date(13)			
Cardholder Name(14)					

Date：_____ Signature (15)：_____

II. Find the following words from the puzzle. One is done for you.

從字謎中找出下列生字

baggage	*voucher*	*registration*	*signature*
passport	*arrival*	*departure*	*guarantee*
nationality	*confirmation*	*vacancy*	*counter*

 文化通

　　旅行中「住」佔了很重要的部分。住宿的品質，除了旅館的硬體設施，還包括服務，若能事先瞭解當地有關旅館住宿的文化，不但不失禮儀，也往往可以享受愉快的住宿經驗。

　　有關旅館的文化差異，除了硬體上因漢文化對「4」的禁忌，旅館通常沒有4樓；在服務上，各地也有不同的情形。在筆者的經驗中，有些國家的4星旅館，check in後會幫客人將行李送到房間，但有些國家則沒有此服務。如在德國，一般4星旅館是沒有行李員，check in 後要自己提行李到房間，除了高級餐廳，一般餐廳大多也是自己進去找位子，沒有帶位。

　　到各國旅行，住宿時常會遇到的問題是，到底要不要放床頭小費、要不要給服務生小費、給多少？在台灣通常已將10%的服務費包含在定價中，給不給小費全憑客人自由決定。一般而言，給小費是對服務人員的肯定與讚許，但有些國家是「一定」要給小費，如果客人「忘了」給，服務生會暗示，甚至明示；有些國家則不收小費，如日本，筆者就遇過，放在床頭的小費，晚上回到房間，還是原封不動的放著。至於小費要給多少才恰當？各地有不同的標準，旅館的等

級、當地的所得及消費水準，都是參考的依據。一般普遍的標準是，行李員及床頭小費約1至2美元，歐元國家則為1至2歐元。

　　所謂入境隨俗，掌握當地的小費文化，有時也會為自己帶來意外的小驚喜。筆者有幾次愉快的經驗，晚上回到住處，床上摺了一隻天鵝、一朵花，或以花瓣排字，每天不同，每天回去都帶著期待。

Egypt Nile Cruise上

Sri Lanka Dambulla Amaya Hotel

Sri Lanka Kandy Queens Hotel

Sri Lanka Polonnaruwa-Sudu Araliya Hotel

Notes

Unit 4

Services & Facilities

服務項目及設施

 單字特區

01 reception
〔rɪˈsɛpʃən〕
接待櫃檯

02 lobby
〔ˈlɑbɪ〕
大廳

03 lift / elevator
〔lɪft〕/〔ˈɛləˌvetɚ〕
電梯

04 restaurant
〔ˈrɛstəˌrant〕
餐廳

05 bar / lounge
〔bɑr〕/〔laʊndʒ〕
酒吧／休閒廳

06 café
〔kæ'fe〕
咖啡廳

07 business center
〔'bɪznəs 'sɛntɚ〕
會議室，商務中心

08 conference room
〔'kɑnfərəns rum〕
會議室

09 banquet hall
〔'bæŋkwɪt hɔl〕
宴會廳

10 gift shop
〔gɪft ʃap〕
禮品店

11 SPA
〔spa〕
水療館

12 gym/gymnasium
〔dʒɪm〕〔dʒɪm'nezɪəm〕
健身房

13 swimming pool
〔'swɪmɪŋ pul〕
游泳池

14 sauna
〔'saʊnə〕
三溫暖

15 steam room
〔stim rum〕
蒸氣浴房

16 internet access
〔'ɪntɚnɛt 'æksɛs〕
網路設施

17 car park
〔kar park〕
停車場

18 accessible facilities
〔æk'sɛsəbl fə'sɪlətɪz〕
無障礙設施

19 casino
〔kə'sɪno〕
賭場（卡西諾）

20 tour desk
〔tur dɛsk〕
旅遊諮詢櫃檯

21 currency exchange
service
〔'kɝənsɪ ɪks'tʃendʒ
'sɝvɪs〕
外幣兌換服務

22 laundry service
〔'lɔndrɪ 'sɝvɪs〕
衣物送洗服務

23 room service
〔rum 'sɝvɪs〕
客房服務

24 babysitting service
〔'bebɪ sɪtɪŋ 'sɝvɪs〕
保姆服務

25 shuttle bus
〔'ʃʌtl̩ bʌs〕
接駁車

26 wake-up service
〔wek ʌp 'sɝvɪs〕
晨喚服務

實用例句

1. reception：接待櫃檯

   （ex）Leave your keys at the reception when going out.

   出去時，請將鑰匙留在接待櫃檯。

2. lift：電梯

   （ex）Please take the lift to the ninth floor.

   請搭電梯到9樓。

3. banquet hall：宴會廳

   （ex）The welcome party is held in the banquet hall on the tenth floor.

   歡迎晚宴在10樓的宴會廳舉辦。

4. internet access：網路設施

   （ex）We offer internet accesses in the business center and WIFI in the lounge.

   商務中心有網路設施，休息室有無線網路。

5. gym：健身房

   （ex）If you don't want to go out for exercise, we have a gym in the hotel.

   如果你不想出去運動，飯店內也有健身房。

6. currency exchange service：外幣兌換服務

（ex）We offer currency exchange service in the hotel. The counter opens from 9:00 a.m. to 3:00 p.m.

飯店提供外幣兌換服務。兌換櫃檯營業時間從早上9點到下午3點。

7. laundry service：衣物送洗服務

（ex）If you need laundry service, just put your laundry in your laundry bag, and then put the Pick Up My Laundry sign on your doorknob.

如果你需要送洗衣物，把衣物放進洗衣袋，再把衣物送洗的牌子掛在門把上就可以了。

8. tour desk：旅遊諮詢

（ex）Go to our tour desk for more information.

欲知更多詳情，請洽旅遊諮詢櫃檯。

9. shuttle bus：接駁車

（ex）The hotel offers free airport pickup service. You can take our shuttle bus at the third terminal.

飯店提供免費機場接送服務。你可以在第三航廈搭我們的接駁車。

10. turndown service：開床服務

    （ex）Clerk: I'm afraid there's an extra charge for turndown service.

        Customer：It's OK. My family and I would like a more comfortable stay with your hotel.

        櫃檯：不好意思，加床服務需要加收額外的費用。

        顧客：沒問題，我們想要在飯店住得更舒適。

11. airport pick-up：機場接送

    （ex）Clerk: Our hotel offers free airport pick-up service. Please go to the concierge for more information if needed.

        Customer：Thank you for the information.

        櫃檯：我們提供免費的機場接送服務。如果有需要，請洽櫃檯。

        顧客：非常感謝您的訊息。

12. babysitting service：保姆服務

    （ex）Customer：I need to go to a meeting this morning, and is there anyone who can look after my baby?

        Clerk：Don't worry, madam. We do offer babysitting service.

        顧客：我今天早上要開會。請問有人可以照顧我的小孩嗎？

        櫃檯：請不用擔心，我們飯店也提供保姆服務。

Other Hotel Services and Facilities　旅館其他服務項目與設施

1. concierge desk	管家服務櫃檯
2. secretarial service	秘書服務
3. airport pick-up	機場接送
4. turndown service	開床服務
5. gym/fitness center	健身房
6. recreation room	娛樂室
7. international phone call service	國際電話服務
8. laundry department	洗衣部
9. accessible facilities = handicapped facilities	無障礙空間
10. wake-up call service = morning call service	晨喚服務
11. postal service	郵件服務
12. surface mail	平信
13. printed matter	印刷品
14. special mail	限時專送
15. fragile	易碎品
16. express mail	快捷郵件
17. airmail	航空郵件
18. registered mail	掛號信

I. Laundry Service 衣物送洗服務

A customer calls the Laundry Department.

Clerk : Good afternoon, Laundry Department. How may I help you?

Customer : Hello, it's Gorge Huang in Room 201. I have a suit and some shirts which need dry-cleaning as soon as possible. Should I send them to the laundry?

Clerk : Certainly, sir. Please write down special instructions on your laundry list. And put your suit and shirts, together with your laundry list, in the dry-cleaning bag, not the laundry bag.

Customer : Thank you very much for the information.

Clerk : You're welcome.

II. Postal Service　郵件服務

A customer is at the reception.

Clerk　　：Good morning, sir. How may I help you?

Customer：I'd like to mail this package. Can you tell me where I can mail it?

Clerk　　：We could send the package for you. Would you like to send it by special delivery or registered mail?

Customer：By registered mail, please.

Clerk　　：I'll weigh it. Please wait a moment. It weighs 1 kilo and costs NT$150.

Customer：Could you charge it to my room bill, please?

Clerk　　：Sure. May I see your room key and some IDs, please?

Customer：Here you are.

I. Complete the following sentences. Use the words as clues. 請根據下表的提示完成句子。

reception,	lift,	banquet hall,
gym,	currency exchange service,	
Internet access,	laundry service,	
tour desk		

1. Customer: Do you offer any _____? I need to change some money.

2. If you have any questions about the city tour, please go to the _____ in our hotel.

3. If you don't want to go jogging, you can stay in the _____. It's next to the swimming pool, on the top floor.

4. Do you have _____ ? I have a lot of dirty clothes.

5. Please do not hesitate to telephone the _____ if you need any further services.

6. The Reception Dinner is held in the _____.

II. Reorder the words.請重新排列下列單字

1. ntpcreeoi   6. snaau

2. gnleuo   7. gmmnsyaiu

3. ccnnrfoeee   8. strmmeaoo

4. ttnrrseaau   9. gftshpio

5. cfaé   10. llhtqnbaaue

文化通

　一般而言，飯店的設施、服務與等級有關，等級愈高的附屬設施通常也較多。對消費者而言，飯店分級提供了選擇飯店的參考與依據，可以依個人需求做選擇。

　全世界並無統一的飯店分級制度與標準，例如美國汽車協會AAA（American Automobile Association）是採鑽石分級系統，從1顆鑽石到5顆，分五個等級。1顆鑽代表所有設施達到所有要求水準，它們是乾淨的、安全的，並且維護良好。5顆鑽代表在設施設備與經營都顯示出超越旅客預期、無懈可擊完美的水準。

　台灣過去是採梅花分級方式，為了與世界接軌，改採國際較普及的星級分級制，2008年交通部觀光局訂定「星級旅館評鑑計畫」，並於2009至2011年完成第一批業者審核。這套星級旅館評鑑，以飯店硬體設施及服務品質來評比，分為1星（one star）至5星（five star）。第一階段先評硬體設施，以完善度給予1至3顆星；通過基礎評鑑，才可進行第二階段服務品質的評比，給予4、5顆星。五星級飯店是最高等級，在設施及服務自然是最高級，在價格上當然也較高。

Notes

Unit 5

Room Types & Room Facilities

房型及設備

單字特區

Part I：Room Types 房型

01 single room
〔'sɪŋgḷ rum〕單人房

02 double room
〔'dʌbḷ rum〕雙人房
（一張大床）

03 twin room〔twɪn rum〕
雙床房（二張小床）

04 triple room〔'trɪpḷ rum〕
三人房

05 family room〔'fæməlɪ
rum〕親子/四人房

06 suite〔swit〕
套房

07 presidential suite
〔͵prɛzə'dɛnʃəl swit〕
總統套房

08 honeymoon suite
〔'hʌnɪ͵mun swit〕
蜜月套房

09 business suite
〔'bɪznɪs swit〕
商務套房

10 standard room
〔'stændɚd rum〕
標準房型

11 deluxe room
〔dɪ'lʌks rum〕
豪華房型

12 superior room
〔su'pɪrɪɚ rum〕
高級客房

13 room with a view
〔rum wɪθ ə vju〕
景觀房

14 room with a balcony
〔rum wɪθ ə 'bælkənɪ〕
有陽台的房間

Part II：Room Facilities 客房設備

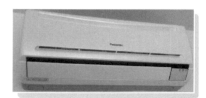

15 air-conditioning
〔ɛr kən'dɪʃənɪŋ〕
空調

16 heater〔'hitɚ〕
暖器

17 cable TV or satellite TV
〔'kebḷ ti vi〕/
〔'sætḷ ˌaɪt ti vi〕
有線電視/衛星電視

18 remote control
〔rɪ'mot kən'trol〕
搖控器

19 pay-per-view movies
〔pe pɝ vju muvɪz〕
按次付費電影

20 wireless Internet access
〔'waɪrləs 'ɪntɚnɛt
'æksɛs〕無線網路

21 telephone〔'tɛləˌfon〕
電話

22 mini bar〔'mɪnɪ bar〕
冰箱，迷你吧檯

23 electric kettle
〔ɪ'lɛktrɪk 'kɛtl̩〕
電熱水壺

24 safe deposit box
〔sef dɪ'pazɪt baks〕
保險箱

25 iron & ironing board
〔'aɪɚn〕〔'aɪɚnɪŋ
bord〕熨斗及熨衣板

26 dresser〔'drɛsɚ〕
梳妝台

27 closet〔'klɑzət〕衣櫃

28 laundry bag
〔'lɔndrɪ bæg〕
洗衣袋

091

29 luggage stand
〔'lʌgɪdʒ stænd〕
行李架

30 hairdryer
〔'hɛr,draɪɚ〕吹風機

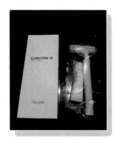

31 electric razor outlet
〔ɪ'lɛktrɪk 'rezɚ
'aʊt,lɛt〕電動刮鬍刀座

32 bathtub〔'bæθ,tʌb〕
浴缸

33 Jacuzzi
〔dʒə'kuzɪ〕
按摩浴缸

34 bidet〔bɪ'de〕
免治馬桶

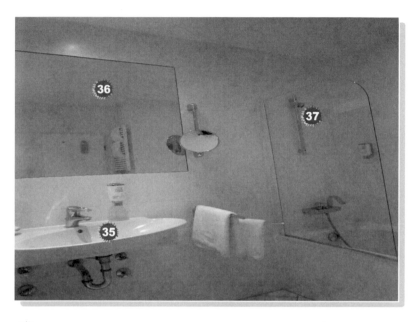

35 wash basin〔waʃ 'besn〕洗臉盆

36 mirror〔'mɪrɚ〕鏡子

37 shower nozzle〔'ʃaʊɚ 'nazl̩〕蓮蓬頭

單字加料區

1. dorm bed/bunk bed——雙層舖/上下舖，許多青年旅社
   提供較便宜的上下舖的住宿，適合預算比較少的背包客
   （backpacker）。
2. baby cot 嬰兒床——若有嬰兒隨行，需在訂房時加註。
3. extra bed/cot 行軍床——若需加床，需在訂房時加註。
4. safe deposit box 亦稱為 room safe 保險箱。

1. single room：單人房

   （ex）Guest：Excuse me. I'd like to reserve a single room for three nights starting April fourth?

   Clerk：Just a minute, madam. I will check availability.

   顧客：您好，我想要訂一間單人房，4月4日起訂3個晚上。

   櫃檯：請稍等，女士，我查一下還有沒有空房。

2. double room：雙人房

   （ex）Guest：Excuse me. How much is a double room in your hotel?

   Clerk：It is NT$3000 per night, but we can give you a 30% discount from Sunday through Thursday night.

   顧客：請問你們飯店的雙人房一晚上多少錢?

   櫃檯：雙人房一個晚上3000元台幣，若您是週日到週四訂房，我們可以打七折。

3. twin room：雙床房

   （ex）Guest：Are there any rooms for two people for tomorrow night?

   Clerk：Yes, we do. We have a double room and a twin room. Which one would you prefer?

   顧客：請問明晚你們有沒有任何2人房的空房?

   櫃檯：我們有雙人房和雙床房，請問您想要訂那一種?

4. closet：衣櫃

（ex）Guest：Excuse me. Can I have another quilt? I feel cold in my room.

Clerk：You can find a spare blanket in the closet. If it's not enough, please let us know.

顧客：請問可以多給我一床棉被嗎？我覺得房裡有點冷。

櫃檯：房間櫃子裡有一條備用的毯子，如果還是不夠，請知會我們。

5. safe deposit box：保險箱

（ex）Guest：Where can I keep some of my valuable personal belongings in the hotel?

Clerk：There is a safe deposit box in the room. You can keep your valuable objects in there.

顧客：請問飯店裡那裡可以寄存重要物品？

櫃檯：房內有保險箱，您可以將重要物品鎖在裡面。

6. shower nozzle：蓮蓬頭

（ex）Guest：Excuse me. This is room 607. The shower nozzle in my room doesn't work.

Clerk：I'm very sorry to hear that, sir. I'll send someone up immediately.

顧客：我這裡是607房，我房裡的蓮蓬頭不能用。

櫃檯：很抱歉，先生，我馬上派人上去處理。

Asking of availability and room facilities
詢問訂房及房內設施

Guest：Excuse me. I'd like to reserve a double room for three nights starting April fourth.

Clerk：Just a minute, ma'am. I will check availability. Yes, ma'am. We still have double rooms. How many nights are you going to reserve?

Guest：Three nights.

Clerk：May I have your name, please?

Guest：Clark. Jenny Clark. Does the room have a Cable TV?

Clerk：Yes, ma'am. It does.

Guest：Does it provide wireless Internet access?

Clerk：Yes, ma'am. All rooms in our hotel are equipped with wireless Internet access. We'll give you the account name and the code upon request.

Guest：Does the room have a Jacuzzi?

Clerk：I'm afraid not. Jacuzzis are only available in suites.

Guest：Does it have a room safe?

Clerk：No, it doesn't. But you can leave your valuables here at the front desk. You can put them in a safety deposit box.

Guest：Thank you very much.

單字考驗區

I. Write down the numbered items in English.

寫出圖片中各項物品的英文。

1 _____   **2** _____

3 _____   **4** _____

5 _____   **6** _____

II. Reorganize the following words and solve the puzzle.

請重新排列組合下列生字，再將標有數字的字母填進方框
以解出字謎。

Hotel Room Facilities

EHTARE	
TEMROE NOTLORC	(with cell numbered 4)
TOLEENEPH	(with cell numbered 6)
NIMI BRA	(with cell numbered 1)
CEREIL TC TEKLET	(with cell numbered 2)
DRSERSE	
COSLET	
HYRIDRERA	(with cells numbered 3 and 7)
RRAZO	
BATTUHB	
ZIAZUCJ	(with cell numbered 5)
BAISN	
RIRMOR	
EDTIB	

F ☐ ☐ ☐ ☐ ☐ ☐ ☐
  1 2 3 4 5 6 7

Unscramble each of the clue words.
Copy the letters in the numbered cells to other cells with the same number.

Created by Puzzlemaker at DiscoveryEducation.com

　　準備行李是一門學問，尤其是自助旅行，如何在該帶的都帶到的情況下減輕行李的重量，除了經驗，事先做功課會有很大的幫助。例如，訂房時先瞭解旅館提供的設備，可以減少帶到用不到的行李。

　　一般旅館房間提供的設備與旅館等級有關，有時也會因文化習俗而不同，例如在亞洲國家的旅館，大多會提供牙膏、牙刷，在歐美國家除了五星旅館，一般三、四星旅館通常是不提供牙膏、牙刷的。其它盥洗用品，浴巾、毛巾、擦手巾、香皂或沐浴乳、衛生紙等基本上都會提供的，梳子、浴帽、刮鬍刀、洗髮乳、乳液、棉花棒、拖鞋、針線包、吹風機等則不一定會有。房間裡除了床，有沒有空調、暖器、冰箱、咖啡機、熱水壺、電視、保險箱、網路等，浴室是淋浴，還是有浴缸，這些在訂房時都可以問清楚或看清楚。

　　此外，訂房時選擇房型，除了單人房、雙人房人數的區分，有的還有床的區分，如雙人房有一張大床（double room）和二張小床（twin room）之分。根據個人習慣，選擇適合的床型，可以讓自己睡得舒服。以下是常見床型的尺寸參考：

King Size Bed，193cm寬×203cm長，是最大尺寸的床
Queen Size Bed，152cm寬×203cm長
Double（Full）Size Bed，137cm寬×190cm長
Twin（Single）Size Bed，99cm寬×190cm長

Notes

Directions & Symbols / Signs

指示方位及標誌

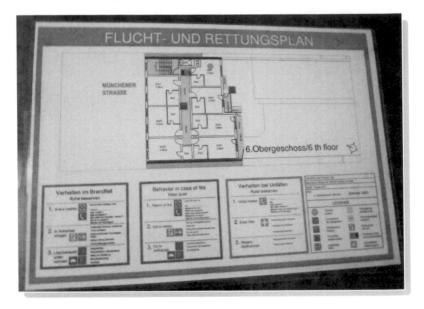

01 floor plan

〔flɔr plæn〕

樓層圖

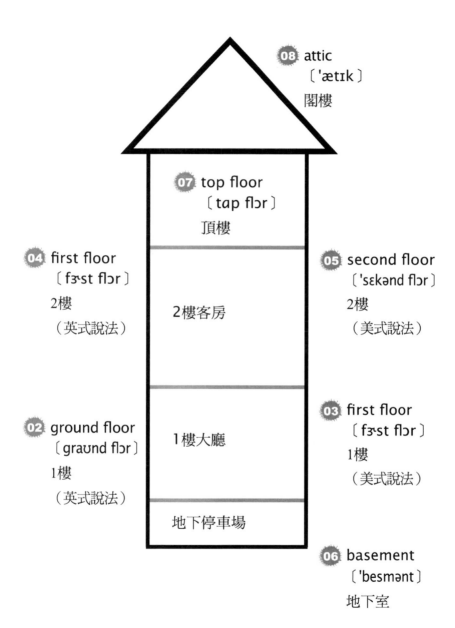

08 attic
〔'ætɪk〕
閣樓

07 top floor
〔tɑp flɔr〕
頂樓

04 first floor
〔fɝst flɔr〕
2樓
（英式說法）

05 second floor
〔'sɛkənd flɔr〕
2樓
（美式說法）

2樓客房

02 ground floor
〔graʊnd flɔr〕
1樓
（英式說法）

03 first floor
〔fɝst flɔr〕
1樓
（美式說法）

1樓大廳

地下停車場

06 basement
〔'besmənt〕
地下室

09 turn right
〔tɝn raɪt〕
右轉

10 turn left
〔tɝn lɛft〕
左轉

11 take the lift
〔tek ðə lɪft〕
搭電梯

12 take the lift to the 3rd
floor
〔tek ðə lɪft tu ðə θɝd
flɔr〕
搭電梯到3樓

13 go straight
〔go stret〕
直走

14 go along
〔go ə'lɔŋ〕
沿著…走

15 on the right/〔ɑn ðə raɪt〕
on the right-hand side
〔ɑn ðə raɪt hænd saɪd〕
在右手邊

16 on the left/〔ɑn ðə lɛft〕
on the left-hand side
〔ɑn ðə lɛft hænd saɪd〕
在左手邊

17 in front of
〔ɪn frʌnt əv〕
在…前面

18 hotel room sign
〔ho'tɛl rum saɪn〕
（hotel room signage）
〔ho'tɛl rum 'saɪnɪdʒ〕
房間指示標示

19 room number sign
〔rum 'nʌmbɚ saɪn〕
房間號碼指示標示

20 exit
〔'ɛksɪt〕
緊急逃生口

21 fire extinguisher
〔faɪr ɪk'stɪŋgwɪʃɚ〕
滅火器

22 emergency
evacuation plan
〔ɪ'mɝ·ʤənsɪ
ɪˌvækjʊ'eʃən plæn〕
避難逃生路線圖

23 toilet
〔'tɔɪlət〕
廁所

24 men's room
〔mɛnz rum〕
男廁

25 women's room
〔'wɪmənz rum〕
女廁

26 Please do not disturb.
〔dɪˈstɝb〕
請勿打擾。

27 Please make up the room now.
〔mek ʌp〕
請整理房間。

1. turn left：左轉

（ex）Guest：Excuse me. Can you tell me how to get to the chemist?

Clerk：Turn left at the intersection, and it's on the right.

顧客：請問藥房怎麼走？

櫃檯：十字路口左轉，就在右手邊。

2. across the hall：大廳的對面

（ex）Guest：Would you tell me where the gift shop is, please?

Clerk：It's just across the hall.

顧客：請問禮品店怎麼走？

櫃檯：就在大廳的對面。

3. take the lift to the third floor：搭電梯到3樓

（ex）Guest：Excuse me. Is there a post office at this mall?

Clerk：Yes, there's one on the third floor. You can take the lift to the third floor. It's across the hall.

顧客：請問這個購物中心有郵局嗎？

櫃檯：三樓有。你要搭電梯到三樓，就在大廳對面。

4. emergency evacuation plan：避難逃生路線圖

（ex）Guest A：What are you looking for?

Guest B：I am looking for the emergency evacuation plan, just in case of emergencies.

顧客A：妳在找什麼？

顧客B：我在找避難逃生路線圖，以防萬一。

5. fire extinguisher：滅火器

（ex）Clerk：Concierge Desk. May I help you?

Guest：Yes, this is Room 201. The fire extinguisher is out of date.

Clerk：Oh, I am so sorry. I will have someone to deal with it.

櫃檯：這是櫃檯，您好。我可以幫上什麼忙嗎？

顧客：這是201號房，房裡的滅火器過期了。

櫃檯：真的很抱歉，我們馬上派人去處理。

6. Please do not disturb. 請勿打擾。

（ex）Guest A：I am really exhausted. I don't want to go to the city tour today. What I want to do is stay in the hotel room.

Guest B：OK, then put the "Please do not disturb." sign on your doorknob.

顧客A：我很累，不想去城市觀光。

顧客B：好吧，那要把「請勿打擾」的牌子掛在門把上。

7. Please make up the room now. 請整理房間。

（ex）Guest：My room needs to be cleaned. It's in a mess.

Clerk：You just put the "Please make up the room now." on the doorknob. The room maid will come to clean it.

顧客：我的房間需要整理，它亂的可以。

櫃檯：那你只需要把「請整理房間」的牌子掛在門把上，房務人員就會來打掃。

I. More Directions　方位

1. go along…	沿著走	
2. next to…	在旁邊	
3. across from	在對面	
4. between… and…	在…與…之間	
5. on the left	在左邊	
6. go straight	直走	
7. go past	經過	
8. take the first right	第一條街右轉	
9. turn right at the bookstore	在書店那右轉	
10. take the second left	第二條街左轉	

11. on the corner of Chung-Shan Road and Chung-Hwa Road

在中山路與中華路轉角

II. Common Words　常用的單字

1. car park = parking lot	停車場	
2. lost and found	失物招領處	
3. stairs	樓梯	
4. upstairs	樓上	
5. drugstore = chemist = pharmacy	藥局	
6. souvenirs	紀念品店	
7. toilets = restrooms	廁所	

8. emergency evacuation plan = fire evacuation plan/ map

避難逃生路線圖

情境對話

Asking Locations　地點

A guest is at the reception and asks the receptionist about the services the hotel offers.

Guest：Excuse me, where's the restaurant, please?

Clerk：It's on the third floor, madam. The stairs are over there on the right, or there's an elevator on the left.

Guest：Then, I'll take the stairs. Oh, yes. Is the cocktail bar on the first floor? Only I can't find it.

Clerk：No, madam. The cocktail bar is on the third floor.

Guest：I see. Thank you. One more thing. I'd like to change some money. Is there an exchange bureau near here?

Clerk：Yes, madam. We do have an exchange bureau, but it opens at 10 a.m.

Guest：OK. Where exactly is it?

Clerk：It's upstairs on the second floor.

單字考驗區

I. Reorder the words. 請重新排列下列單字。

1. txie   _____

2. letiot   _____

3. ngis   _____

4. aeeolrvt   _____

5. eflt   _____

6. iubdrst   _____

7. eeecgmnry   _____

8. aaeioucntv   _____

II. What do these symbols mean? Please write down their English.

請根據下列圖示寫出英文。

1 _____

2 _____

3 _____

4 _____

5 _____

6 _____

III. Use the words in the box and complete the sentences.

請根據下列提示完成句子。

> fire extinguisher, emergency evacuation plan,
>
> Please do not disturb. car park,
>
> Please make up the room now.

1. The thing used to put out the fire is called a _____.

2. After entering your room, the first thing to do is to check out the _____, in case there is an emergency.

3. When you require the housemaids to clean your room, please put the _____ sign on the doorknob.

4. Customer: Excuse me. Do you have a _____? I will drive to your hotel.

5. If you prefer to rest in your room without any disturbance, please put the _____ sign on the doorknob.

旅行時，學幾句當地基本的打招呼用語，可以拉近距離，多幾分親切。一句「Good Morning」、「おはよ」、「bonjour」，是美好一天的開始。

除了「你好」、「早安」、「謝謝」，有一個旅行中很實用的字，就是「廁所」。英文「toilet」或「restroom」在多數西方國家行得通，但在非英語系地區，或語言不通時，符號或圖示，就會是最簡易也最有效的溝通。

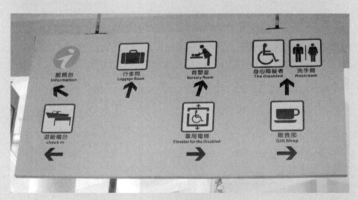

以下是幾種常見廁所的符號標示：

GENTS   LADIES

MEN   WOMEN

Toilet, restroom, WC

人形（女著裙，男著褲）

高跟鞋vs煙斗

　　圖示是跨越語言最原始的表達，在筆者的旅行經
驗中，有些地方的商店招牌用圖示，店家發揮創意，
形成有趣吸引人的觀光景觀。

Spain Cordoba 小巷

Austria Salzburg

Germany Rothunburg

Germany Rothunburg

Notes

Unit 7

Housekeeping

房務設備

Part I：Janitorial Supplies　房務清潔用品

  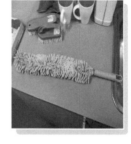

01 mop
〔mɑp〕拖把

02 dust control
mop〔dʌst
kənˈtrol
mɑp〕
除塵拖把

03 scrubber
〔ˈskrʌbɚ〕
刷子，擦布

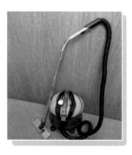  

05 stripper
〔ˈstrɪpɚ〕
強效清潔劑

06 squeegee
〔ˈskwidʒi〕
橡皮刮板

04 vacuum
cleaner
〔ˈvækjuəm
ˈklinɚ〕
吸塵器

08 cornice
〔'kɔrnɪs〕
網狀毛刷

07 air freshener
〔ɛr 'frɛʃənɚ〕
空氣清新劑

09 spot remover
〔spat rɪ'muvɚ〕
去汙劑

11 housekeeping cart
〔'haʊs'kipɪŋ kart〕
清潔推車

10 polishing machine
〔'palɪʃɪŋ mə'ʃin〕
磨光機

Part II：Common Supplies in Guest Room　客房常見用品

12 tea bag/ coffee bag
〔ti bæg〕;〔'kɔfɪ bæg〕
茶包；咖啡包

13 teaspoon
〔'ti,spun〕
湯匙

14 saucer〔'sɔsɚ〕
杯碟

15 coaster〔'kostɚ〕
杯墊

16 cup〔'kʌp〕
咖啡杯

17 mineral water
〔'mɪnərəl 'wɔtɚ〕
礦泉水

18 ashtray
〔'æʃtre〕
菸灰缸

19 memo paper
〔'mɛmo 'pepɚ〕
便條紙

20 envelop
〔'ɛnvəˌləp〕信封

21 facial tissues
〔'feʃəl
'tɪʃʊz〕面紙

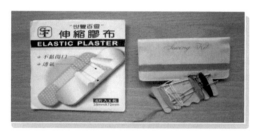

22 band aid
〔bænd ed〕
OK繃

23 sewing kit
〔'soɪŋ kɪt〕
針線包

24 hanger〔'hæŋɚ〕
衣架

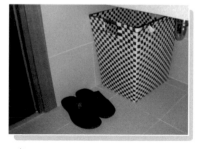

25 slippers〔'slɪpɚz〕
拖鞋

Part III：Bedding Items　床組用品

26 pillow〔'pɪlo〕枕頭

27 sheet〔ʃit〕床單

28 mattress〔'mætrəs〕
床墊

29 quilt〔kwɪlt〕被子

30 blanket〔'blæŋkɪt〕
毯子

Part IV：Bathroom Supplies　浴室用品

31 face towel
〔fes 'taʊəl〕擦臉的毛巾

32 hand towel
〔hænd 'taʊəl〕擦手巾

33 bath towel
〔bæθ 'taʊəl〕浴巾

34 floor towel
〔flor 'taʊəl〕地板巾

35 bathrobe〔'bæθˌrob〕
浴袍；浴衣

36 soap〔sop〕香皂

37 toothpaste
〔'tuθˌpest〕牙膏

38 toothbrush
〔`tuθˌbrʌʃ〕牙刷

39 shower cap
〔'ʃaʊɚ kæp〕浴帽

40 comb〔kom〕梳子

41 Q tips
〔kju tɪps〕棉花棒

42 dental floss
〔'dɛntḷ flɔs〕牙線

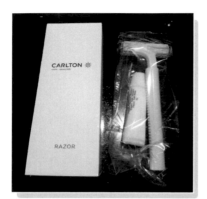

43 razor〔'rezɚ〕
刮鬍刀

44 toilet paper
〔'tɔɪlət 'pepɚ〕衛生紙

45 shampoo
〔ʃæm'pu〕
洗髮精

46 hair conditioner
〔hɛr kən 'dɪʃənɚ〕
潤髮乳

47 shower gel
〔'ʃaʊɚ dʒɛl〕沐浴精

48 body lotion〔'badɪ 'loʃən〕
乳液

圖解旅館英文詞彙

實用例句

1. squeegee：橡皮刮板

（ex）Use the squeegee to remove the stains from the window.
利用橡皮刮板將窗戶上的汙漬清除乾淨。

2. air freshener：空氣清新劑

（ex）You can use some air freshener to get rid of bad smells.
你可以用一些空氣清新劑來消除臭味。

3. memo paper：便條紙（又可稱note paper/ memo card/ memo pads）

（ex）I am used to take down some important schedules on the memo paper.
我習慣將一些重要行程記在便條紙上。

4. mineral water：礦泉水（又可稱spring water）

（ex）There's no mineral water in the minibar. Could you send someone to restock it?
小冰箱裡沒有礦泉水了。你可以找人來補一下嗎？

5. ashtray：菸灰缸

（ex）Be sure to empty the garbage cans and ashtrays in the lobby.
務必將大廳裡的垃圾桶和菸灰缸清乾淨。

6. band aid：OK繃

（ex）I just cut my finger, and it's bleeding. Do you have medical alcohol and band aids?

我剛剛切到手指，現在還在流血。你有藥用酒精和OK繃嗎？

7. pillow：枕頭

（ex）I am allergic to feather. Can I have a foam pillow?

我對羽毛過敏。可不可以給我一個乳膠枕？

8. sheet：床單

（ex）I spilt some coffee on the sheets. Would it be possible to have them changed?

我不小心把咖啡灑到床單上，可以幫我換新的嗎？

9. quilt：被子

（ex）It's been cold all day. I need an extra quilt.

今天一整天都很冷，我需要多一件被子。

10. floor towel：地板巾

（ex）The faucet keeps leaping. There is water all over the bathroom floor. We need some extra floor towels.

水龍頭一直在漏水，浴室地板都是水，我們需要一些地板巾。

11. shower gel：沐浴精（又可稱body shampoo, bath gel）

（ex）My daughter needs to take a bath. Do you have shower
gel for babies?

我女兒要洗澡，你們有嬰兒用的沐浴精嗎？

12. toilet paper：衛生紙

（ex）There's no toilet paper in my bathroom. Could you send
a housekeeper to bring it up？

浴室沒有衛生紙了，你可以叫房務員送過來嗎?

Asking Permission to clean rooms　詢問是否可以整房

Housekeeper：*(knocking on the door)* Housekeeping!

Guest　　　：*(opening the door)* Yes.

Housekeeper：I'm sorry to disturb you, ma'am. Would you like your room cleaned now?

Guest　　　：No, not right now.

Housekeeper：Would you like your towels changed?

Guest　　　：No, not really. Oh, wait. I think the sheets need to be changed. I accidentally spilt some tea on them.

Housekeeper：No problem. I will change them right away.

Guest　　　：Thank you.

Asking when to clean rooms　請問何時可以整房

Housekeeper：*(knocking on the door)* Housekeeping!

Guest　　　：Oh, what is it?

Housekeeper：Sorry to disturb you, sir. May we clean your room now?

Guest　　　：My kid is taking a shower. Can you come back later?

Housekeeper：What time would be convenient, sir?

Guest　　　：Could you come again 30 minutes later?

Housekeeper：Yes.

Laundry Service　洗衣服務

Housekeeper：Housekeeping. Angel's speaking. How may I help you?

Guest 　　　: I have two dresses that need to be washed. Could you send someone to pick up my laundry?

Housekeeper：Yes. What is your room number?

Guest 　　　: Room 1125.

Housekeeper：1125? OK, please fill out the laundry list and put it in the bag.

Guest 　　　: OK.

Housekeeper：Leave the bag behind the door. I'll send someone right up in 10 minutes.

Guest 　　　: Thank you.

Supply Things　提供房間用品

Housekeeper：Housekeeping. This is Angel speaking. May I help you?

Guest 　　　: Yes. There's no toilet paper in my bathroom.

Housekeeper：I'm terribly sorry. May I have your name and room number, please?

Guest 　　　: I'm Jessica Adams in Room 1225.

Housekeeper：Yes, Ms. Adams. I'll get a housekeeper to bring it up.

Guest 　　　: Thank you. And could I have some more hand towels?

Housekeeper：Certainly, Ms. Is there anything else?

Guest 　　　: No. That'll be all. Thank you.

Housekeeper：You're welcome. Thank you for calling.

單字考驗區

I. Name the following items.請寫出下列物品的英文。

1 _____

2 _____

3 _____

4 _____

5 _____

6 _____

7 _____

8 _____

9 _____

II. Cross out one word in each group that doesn't belong.

請刪除性質不同的單字。

1.	sheet	quilt	slippers	pillow
2.	hand towel	shower gel	ashtray	shampoo
3.	shampoo	stripper	scrubber	squeegee
4.	dental floss	saucer	teaspoon	coaster
5.	shower cap	slippers	shampoo	shower gel
6.	mattress	blanket	sheet	band aids
7.	scrubber	mop	comb	cornice
8.	shower cap	bathrobe	bath towel	saucer

在環保意識愈來愈受到重視的趨勢下，飯店業者亦以省水、省電、減少浪費，追求綠色飯店為目標。除了飯店業者在硬體和服務上做到綠能、環保，也邀請房客一起環保愛地球，例如自己帶盥洗用具，連續住宿不換床單、毛巾，有些飯店會在房間或浴室放置重複使用毛巾或床單的提醒標示，甚至有飯店以續住不換床單、浴巾享有優惠來作為鼓勵。

WE CARE ABOUT THE ENVIRONMENT
We are committed to undertaking practices that preserve our natural resources.

Your bed linens are fresh when you arrive and your room is serviced every day.
For extended stays, your linens will be changed every third day.
However, we are delighted to meet your needs by changing linens upon your request.

LEAVING THIS CARD ON YOUR BED MEANS:
" Please change my bed linens today."

Working together, we can conserve millions of liters of water, save energy and minimize the release of detergents into the environment.
Thank you and enjoy your stay!

我們關注環境
我們致力以實際行動保護自然資源。

當您入住酒店時，您的床單是乾淨的，我們並會每天打掃房間。在您住宿期間，床單將會每三天更換一次。當然，我們亦很樂意按照您的要求隨時為您更換。

擱此卡放在床上表示：
「今天請更換我的床單。」

我們共同努力，便可以節省數以百萬升的水及能源，並且能夠盡量減少清潔劑對環境的污染。

感謝您，希望您住宿愉快！

RENAISSANCE.
HARBOUR VIEW HOTEL
HONG KONG
香港萬麗海景酒店

　　世界一些國家目前都有綠色旅館認證制度，如丹麥的綠色鑰匙、加拿大的綠葉旅館、美國的綠色標籤和大陸的綠色飯店評等制度。位於斯里蘭卡丹布拉市（Dambulla）的Kandalama旅館被美國綠色建築協會（USGBC）評為全球第一座LEED（Leadship in Energy & Environment Design）環保旅館，也是亞洲地區第一家獲得「21世紀綠色地球標章」的旅館。

　　Kandalama旅館由知名的斯里蘭卡國寶級建築大師吉奧佛列・巴瓦（Geoffrey Bawa）所設計，於1991年建成。旅館蓋在巨石下，依附山形，從「大門」穿越山洞，進入大廳，開放式的走道、大堂及裸露的岩石，自然的呈現，有別於一般五星旅館華麗的裝潢陳設，完全感覺不到是「在旅館裡」。坐在咖啡廳喝午茶，有湖光山色與松鼠、鳥兒為伴，天氣好時還可遙望20公里遠的千年古蹟獅子岩（Sigiriya），筆者造訪時，還幸運地看到斯里蘭卡國鳥黑尾原雞（學名 *Gallus lafayetii*）。

Notes

Notes

Unit 8

Restaurant & Bar

餐廳與酒吧

Part I：Breakfast 早餐

01 traditional style breakfast
〔trə'dɪʃənḷ staɪl 'brɛkfəst〕
傳統式早餐

02 western style breakfast
〔'wɛstɚn staɪl 'brɛkfəst〕
西式早餐

03 buffet〔bə'fe〕自助式

04 salad bar〔'sæləd bar〕
沙拉吧

05 toast〔tost〕吐司

06 croissant
〔krwɑ'sɑnt〕
牛角麵包

07 baguet
〔bæ'gɛt〕
法國麵包

08 bun
〔bʌn〕
餐包

09 cake〔kek〕蛋糕

10 butter
〔'bʌtɚ〕
奶油

11 jam
〔dʒæm〕
果醬

12 cheese
〔tʃiz〕
起司

13 sausage
〔'sɔsɪdʒ〕
香腸

14 bacon〔'bekən〕培根

15 ham〔hæm〕火腿

16 sunny-side up
〔'sʌnɪ saɪd ʌp〕
太陽蛋

17 boiled egg
〔bɔɪld ɛg〕水煮蛋

18 scrambled egg
〔ˌskræmbḷd 'ɛg〕炒蛋

19 fried egg〔fraɪd ɛg〕
煎蛋

20 omelet
〔'ɑmlɪt〕蛋餅，蛋捲

21 tomato
〔tə'meto〕番茄

22 hash browns
〔hæʃ braʊnz〕
薯餅

23 cereal〔'sɪrɪəl〕
玉米片

24 yoghurt〔'jogɚt〕
優格

25 fruit
〔frut〕
水果

26 milk〔mɪlk〕牛奶

27 coffee〔'kɔfɪ〕咖啡

28 tea〔ti〕
茶

29 juice〔dʒus〕
果汁

Part II：Bar 吧檯

30 ice cube〔aɪs kjub〕
冰塊

31 cocktail〔'kaktel〕
雞尾酒

32 brandy〔ˈbrændɪ〕
白蘭地

33 whisky〔ˈhwɪskɪ〕
威士忌

34 tequila〔təˈkɪlə〕
龍舌蘭

35 rum
〔rʌm〕
蘭姆酒

36 vodka
〔ˈvɑdkə〕
伏特加

37 gin
〔gɪn〕
琴酒

實用例句

1. buffet：自助式

(ex) The restaurant offers a breakfast buffet.

這家餐廳提供自助式早餐。

2. fried egg：煎蛋

(ex) Waiter：How would you like your fried eggs?

Customer：Sunny-side up, please.

服務生：請問您要點哪一種煎蛋？

顧客：太陽蛋。

3. scrambled egg：炒蛋

(ex) Waiter：What would you like for breakfast?

Customer：Two scrambled eggs, please.

服務生：請問您早餐要吃什麼？

顧客：兩份炒蛋。

4. hash brown：薯餅

(ex) Customer A：What are you having? They look delicious.

Customer B：Hash browns.

顧客A：你在吃什麼？看起來很好吃的樣子。

顧客B：我在吃薯餅。

5. cocktail：雞尾酒

（ex）Bartender：What can I get for you this evening?

Customer：Can you recommend a cocktail?

調酒師：今天晚上您要喝什麼？

顧客：你可以推薦一種雞尾酒嗎？

6. vodka: 伏特加

（ex）Customer：Is it with vodka? I'm allergic to it.

Bartender：No, only with gin.

顧客：裡面加了伏特加嗎？我會過敏。

調酒師：裡面沒有加伏特加，只有琴酒而已。

7. whisky：威士忌

（ex）Customer：A double whisky, on the rocks.

Bartender：Coming up.

顧客：雙份威士忌，加冰塊。

調酒師：馬上來。

8. croissant：可頌麵包

（ex）Customer A：The croissants here are famous. See, there's a long line outside the shop.

Customer B：Wow!

顧客A：這裡的可頌麵包很有名。瞧！外面隊伍已經排很長了。

顧客B：哇！

 單字補給站

I. Types of Western Breakfast　西式早餐的種類

1. American Breakfast美式早餐：

bacon	培根
poached or fried eggs	水波蛋或煎蛋
tomatoes	番茄
mushrooms	香菇
bread or toast	麵包或吐司
sausages	香腸
cornflakes	玉米片
tea／coffee	茶／咖啡
juice	果汁
fruit	水果

2. Continental Breakfast歐式早餐：

croissants	可頌麵包
rolls	麵包捲
bread	麵包
butter	奶油
jam	果醬
coffee／tea	咖啡／茶
juice	果汁

II. Types of eggs　蛋料理的種類

1. fried eggs	煎蛋
fried egg sunny-side up	太陽蛋

fried egg over easy	半熟
fried egg hard	全熟
2. boiled eggs	水煮蛋
hard-boiled egg	全熟
soft-boiled egg	半熟
3. omelet	恩力蛋；蛋包；蛋捲
4. scrambled eggs	炒蛋
5. poached eggs	水波蛋

III. Common equipments used at the bar　吧檯常用的器具

1. stirrer	攪拌棒
2. bar spoon	吧叉匙
3. cocktail strainer	濾冰器
4. ice tongs	夾子
5. jigger	量酒器
6. shaker	搖酒器／雪克杯
7. ice bucket	冰桶
8. Collins glass	可林杯
9. cocktail glass	雞尾酒杯
10. highball glass	高球杯
11. carafe	公杯
12. champagne glass	香檳杯
13. coaster	杯墊

情境對話

A guest is at the restaurant, placing orders.
單點菜單點餐

Waiter：Good morning, sir. Would you like to order from the à la carte menu?

Guest　：Yes, please.

Waiter：Here's our à la carte menu.

Guest　：Thank you.

Waiter：Could I take your order now?

Guest　：Oh, yes. I'd like cornflakes with milk, eggs and two pieces of toast with butter, please.

Waiter：How would you like your eggs? Scrambled or fried?

Guest　：Fried. Sunny-side up, please.

Waiter：And how about your toast? Light or dark?

Guest　：Light, please.

Waiter：So that's cornflakes with milk, fried egg sunny-side up and two pieces of toast with butter, light.

Guest　：That's right.

Waiter：Your order won't be long, sir.

A guest is ordering food at the restaurant.
套餐菜單點餐

Waitress ： Good morning, sir.

Guest 　　 ： Good morning.

Waitress ： Here's our menu.

Guest 　　 ： Do you have an à la carte menu?

Waitress ： I'm sorry. We only have a set menu.

Guest 　　 ： Oh, that's all right.

Waitress ： Are you ready to order now?

Guest 　　 ： Not yet. What would you recommend? The English breakfast or the Continental breakfast?

Waitress ： Well, if you'd like a rich breakfast, the English breakfast is a good choice. We have eggs, croissants, sausages, bacon, cornflakes, orange juice, and coffee included in the English breakfast.

Guest 　　 ： Sounds great. Then I'll have that.

Waitress ： Smart choice. Is there anything else?

Guest 　　 ： Oh, yes. May I have it as smaller portion? I'm afraid that will be too much for me.

Waitress ： Certainly, sir. I'll bring your order soon.

I. Use the words in the box and complete the breakfast menu.

請根據提示，完成下面的菜單。

Cereals, American breakfast, Coffee, Continental breakfast, Jam, Scrambled,

THTC Café

BREAKFAST MENU

1. _____.

   Fresh Juice

   Breakfast Rolls with Jam

2. _____ or Tea

3. _____

   A Choice of Fruit Juices

   (Apple, Grapefruit, Orange, Guava or Tomato)

   A Selection of Bakery Basket

   (Bagel, Croissant, Danish Pastries, Rolls or Toast)

   Served with 4._____ , Butter, or Marmalade

   Fresh Eggs

   Any style (Boiled, 5._____,
   Poached, Fried) with your choice of
   Bacon or Ham

   A Selection of 6._____

   (Corn Flakes, Rice Crispy or Raisin Bran)

   Choice of Beverages

   (Coffee, Decaf Coffee, Tea with Milk or Cream)

II. Use the clues in the box and complete the dialogs.

請根據提示，完成下列的對話，並注意大小寫。

> Western style breakfast, American style breakfast,
> butter, sausage, mushroom,
> scrambled eggs, hash browns

1. Waiter：What would you like for breakfast?

   Guest ：I'd like something heavy, and something hot. And I prefer meat. What would you recommend?

   Waiter：Then I would suggest our 1._____.

2. Waiter：How would you like your toast?

   Guest ：With 2._____, please.

3. Guest ：Excuse me, what are 3._____?

   Waiter：Actually they are fried potatoes, with triangle, rectangular or oval shapes.

4. Guest ：I'd like some eggs for breakfast.

   Waiter：How would you like your eggs?

   Guest ：4._____, please.

　　愉快的早餐是一日美好的開始。訂房時要先瞭解費用是否包含早餐，是西式早餐（western style breakfast）或傳統式早餐（traditional style breakfast），西式早餐又分美式早餐（American breakfast）及歐陸早餐（Continental breakfast）。

　　從飲食來認識一個地方的文化，傳統式早餐是不錯的選擇。日本傳統早餐包括米飯、醃製醬菜、烤鰻魚、味噌湯等。斯里蘭卡傳統早餐一定有pittu（米磨成粉加椰子蒸熟像發糕的一種傳統食物）和咖哩沾醬。如果擔心吃不慣，西式早餐是安全的選擇。

　　一般旅館提供的西式早餐大多區分為美式及歐陸二種，這二種早餐粗略的分別是，美式早餐有熱食，種類多，較豐盛，又稱全早餐（full breakfast）；歐陸早餐則除了咖啡和茶是熱的，其它都是冷食，又稱簡單早餐。歐式早餐的內容一般包括咖啡或茶、果汁、麵包、奶油、果醬。美式早餐的內容則豐盛多了，除了歐式早餐的麵包、奶油、果醬，還有蔬菜沙拉、水煮蛋、炒蛋、蛋捲各式蛋類、培根、香腸、起司、穀物麥片、牛奶、優格、果汁、水果等。若要再細分，西式早餐還有英式、德式、義式⋯等，典型的英式早

餐包括烤蕃茄、磨菇、焗豆、培根或香腸、煎蛋或炒蛋、黑布丁（black pudding）、麵包（可頌或土司）、咖啡或英式早茶（early tea），食量再大，也可以被餵得飽飽飽。

日式早餐

斯里蘭卡傳統早餐

英式早餐

Notes

Unit 9

Complaints, Problems & Requests

抱怨、問題與要求

單字特區

01 What needs to be fixed?
有甚麼需要修理嗎？

Part I：Problems with the Bathroom　浴室問題

02 The sink is clogged.
洗臉槽塞住了。

03 The faucet keeps dripping.
水龍頭一直漏水。

04 The toilet doesn't flush.
馬桶不能沖水。

05 The ceiling light keeps flickering.
燈一直閃不停。

06 The hot water is not hot enough.
熱水不夠熱。

Part II：Room Problems　房間問題

07 My room wasn't made up this morning.
我的房間沒有整理。

08 The TV is out of order.
電視機壞了。

09 My bedside lamp doesn't work.
我的床頭燈不會亮。

10 There is no Internet connection.
沒有網路連線。

Part III：Requests　要求

11 Could I have three cans of Taiwan beer and two packs of potato chips?
可以給我三罐台灣啤酒和兩包洋芋片嗎？

12 I'm still waiting for my luggage.
我還在等我的行李。

實用例句

1. clogged：堵塞（也可以說stopped up）

　（ex）Guest：The plughole in the bathtub is clogged up with hair.

　　　　Clerk：I'll send a housekeeper right away.

　　　　顧客：浴缸裡的出水孔被毛髮堵住了。

　　　　櫃檯：我會請房務員馬上去處理。

2. keep dripping：一直漏水

　（ex）Guest：The toilet keeps dripping all night, and the noise keeps me awake.

　　　　Clerk：I'll seed a plumber right away.

　　　　顧客：馬桶整晚一直漏水，我被吵得不能睡覺。

　　　　櫃檯：我會請水管工馬上過去處理。

3. not flush：不能沖水

　（ex）Guest：The bidet doesn't flush.

　　　　Clerk：I'm sorry for the inconvenience. I'll send a plumber to fix it.

　　　　顧客：免治馬桶不能沖水。

　　　　櫃檯：很抱歉造成您的不便，我會請水管工過去修理。

4. keep flickering：一直閃爍不停

　（ex）Guest：The light bulb of the lamp keeps flickering.

　　　　Clerk：I'll send a repairperson to change it.

　　　　顧客：檯燈的燈泡一直閃爍不停。

　　　　櫃檯：我會請工人過去換燈泡。

5. out of order：壞了（也可以說not work）

　（ex）Guest：The hairdryer in my room is out of order.

　　　　Clerk：I'll have someone bring you a new one right away.

　　　　顧客：房間裡的吹風機壞了。

　　　　櫃檯：我會馬上派人送新的吹風機過去。

6. There is no…：沒有

　（ex）Guest：There is no hot water in the bathroom.

　　　　Clerk：I'll contact maintenance immediately.

　　　　顧客：浴室裡沒有熱水。

　　　　櫃檯：我會馬上與維修部門聯繫。

7. Could I have…?：可以給我…嗎？

　（ex）Guest：Could I have a glass of mineral water?

　　　　Clerk：Sure. Coming right up.

　　　　顧客：可以給我一杯礦泉水嗎？

　　　　櫃檯：好的，馬上送來。

Complaints　抱怨

1. The lightbulb is burned out.
   燈泡燒壞了。

2. The chair is wobbling.
   椅子一直搖晃。

3. My bedside lamp is broken.
   我的床頭燈破掉了。

4. There is a smell of smoke.
   房間有煙味。

5. The toilet is stopped up. It smells.
   馬桶堵住了，很臭。

6. The sheets are filthy.
   被單很髒。

7. The room service breakfast is late.
   早餐還沒送來。

8. My laundry hasn't been sent back yet.
   我送洗的衣物還沒送回來。

9. The people next door are making a lot of noise.
   隔壁房間的人太吵了。

I. Match the problem with the hotel department which is responsible. 請將下列問題與負責處理的旅館部門配對。

1. ____No towels in the bathroom.

2. ____My laundry hasn't been returned.

3. ____My bags haven't been brought to my room.

4. ____The air conditioning isn't working.

5. ____Breakfast hasn't arrived.

6. ____Noisy party in the next room.

A. Bell desk.

B. Room service

C. Housekeeping

D. Landry Desk

E. Maintenance

F. Security

II. How would you deal with the following situations? 請回答如何處理下列情形。

1. The hair dryer in the bathroom doesn't work.

_____

2. The ceiling lights have burned out.

_____

3. The toilet won't flush.

_____

4. I am still waiting for my luggage.

    _____

5. The people next door are making a lot of noise.

    _____

6. The bathroom door doesn't lock.

    _____

III. Fill the following words or phrases in the postcard from Juliet
    to her friend. 請完成下列短文。

keeps dripping	filthy	not working
noisy	refilled	smell of smoke

Hi Cindy

I'm staying at the Paradise Hotel here in Seattle, but it's like a
hell. The room has a _____(1) . The sheets are _____(2). The
showerhead _____(3) and the air-conditioning is _____(4). The
noise keeps me awake all night. The minibar hasn't been _____(5),
so I have to buy drinks from a vending machine. And I can't even
call the front desk clerk because the phone is _____(6)!

Juliet

文化通

　　出國旅行，事先做好功課，往往可以避免一些困擾及問題，例如先瞭解要前往地區使用的電壓及插座，免得自己帶的電器設備不能用或燒壞了，一定會很掃興。台灣的電子設備多使用2孔扁平型，AC110電壓，如果到了電壓或插座不同的地區，就不能使用了！當然，可以向旅館求助，但有的旅館並沒有提供這類的服務，若能自己帶著轉接插頭及電壓轉換器，就可萬無一失。建議攜帶小巧輕便的萬用插座，適用於世界各地主要使用的插座。

　　世界各地的電壓主要有AC110和AC220二種，插座則有2孔扁平型、2孔圓型、3孔扁平型、3孔圓型等多種。

　　此外，住宿時，先看清楚房間裡的東西那些是免費，那些要付費？不想被打擾時、出門時在門口掛上牌子，都可避免不必要的困擾發生。

　　筆者在國外旅行時，看過一些「請打掃、請勿打擾」的掛牌十分有趣，即使看不懂上面的文字，從圖形也絕對能判斷。

Notes

Notes

Unit 10

Paying Bills

CURRENCY EXCHANGE　GELDWECHSEL

ice

付款與帳單

01 cash〔kæʃ〕現金

02 currency rate
〔'kɝənsɪ ret〕匯率

03 New Taiwan Dollar
〔nju 'taɪwan 'dalɚ〕新台幣

04 Chinese Renminbi
〔'tʃaɪ'niz 'rɛn'mɪn'bi〕
人民幣

05 Hong Kong Dollar
〔'haŋ'kaŋ 'dalɚ〕
港幣

06 Japanese Yen
〔͵dʒæpəˈniz jɛn〕
日幣

07 US Dollar
〔ˈdɑlɚ〕美金

08 Euro
〔ˈjʊro〕歐元

09 Vietnam Dong
〔vjɛtˈnæm dɑŋ〕
越南盾

10 credit card
〔'krɛdɪt kard〕
信用卡

11 Master card
〔'mæstɚ kard〕
萬事達卡

12 JCB card
JCB卡

13 Visa〔'vizə〕
威士卡

14 American Express
〔ə'mɛrɪkən ɪk'sprɛs〕
美國運通卡

176

15 bill/check
〔bɪl〕〔tʃɛk〕
帳單

16 statement
〔'stetmənt〕
帳單明細

17 receipt
〔rɪ'sit〕收據

18 invoice
〔'ɪnvɔɪs〕發票

19 discount
〔'dɪskaʊnt〕折扣

20 service charge
〔'sɝvɪs tʃɑrdʒ〕
服務費

21 VAT 增值稅

---

22 tax〔tæks〕稅

23 member/ membership
〔'mɛmbɚ〕
〔'mɛmbɚʃɪp〕
會員

實用例句

1. cash：現金

　　（ex）Cashier：How would you like to pay?

　　　　　Guest：By credit card.

　　　　　出納：請問您要怎麼付帳？

　　　　　顧客：刷卡。

2. credit card：信用卡

　　（ex）Cashier：May I have your credit card, please?

　　　　　Guest：Here you are.

　　　　　出納：請給我您的信用卡。

　　　　　顧客：在這。

3. receipt：收據

　　（ex）Cashier：Here are your receipt and change.

　　　　　Guest：Keep the change.

　　　　　出納：這是您的收據跟零錢。

　　　　　顧客：不用找零了。

4. service charge：服務費

　　（ex）Guest：Is there a service charge?

　　　　　Cashier：Yes. We take a 10% service charge.

　　　　　顧客：請問你們有加收服務費嗎？

　　　　　出納：是的，我們加收一成的服務費。

5. tax：稅

（ex）Guest：How much shall I pay?

Cashier：It's $250, including tax.

顧客：總共多少錢？

出納：含稅總共是250元。

6. membership：會員

（ex）Guest：Is there a discount for membership?

Cashier：Yes. 10% discount for membership.

顧客：請問會員有打折嗎？

出納：是的。會員打九折。

7. invoice：發票

（ex）Cashier：Please keep the invoice for the Uniform-invoice Prize Winning.

Guest：All right. Thank you.

出納：請保留發票以便兌獎。

顧客：好的，謝謝。

8. bill：帳單

（ex）Guest：I'd like to settle my bill, please.

Cashier：Sir, your bill comes to NT $590.

顧客：我要結帳。

出納：先生，總共臺幣590元。

9. American Express：美國運通卡

（ex）Guest：Do you take American Express?

Cashier：Sorry, we only accept VISA and Master card.

顧客：請問你們接受美國運通卡。

出納：不好意思，我們只接受威士卡跟萬事達卡。

10. statement：帳單明細

（ex）Guest：Excuse me, there are some problems with my bill.

Cashier：That's all right. I will go through the statement with you, sir.

顧客：不好意思，我的帳單有問題。

出納：沒關係，我們來對一次帳單。

11. currency rate：匯率

（ex）Guest：I'd like to change New Taiwan Dollars into US Dollars. What's the currency rate?

Cashier：29 NT dollars into 1US dollar, sir.

顧客：我要換美金。請問匯率多少？

出納：29塊臺幣兌1美元。

單字補給站

I. Methods of payment　付款方式

1.By cash.	付現
2.By credit card.	刷卡
3.By traveler's check.	付旅行支票

II. Additional Words其他單字

1.check out	退房
2.currency	貨幣
3.settle	支付、結算
4.payment	支付款項
5.altogether	全部、合計
6.cash register	收銀機
7.credit card terminal	刷卡機
8.bill= check= tab	帳單
9.change	零錢
10.coin	錢幣
11. amount	總額、數量
12. slip	信用卡簽單
13. sign	簽名
14. cashier	收銀員；出納
15. calculator	計算機
16. dotted line	虛線
17. bank draft	銀行匯票

18. wire transfer　　　　　　電匯
19. Korean Won　　　　　　韓幣
20. Thai Baht　　　　　　泰銖
21. British Pound　　　　　英鎊
22. traveler's check　　　　旅行支票
23. personal check　　　　個人信用支票
24. tip　　　　　　　　　　小費
25. tip box　　　　　　　　小費箱
26. statement = bill breakdown　帳單明細

情境對話

I. Paying by credit card　刷卡結帳

A customer is checking out.

Customer：I'd like to check out.

Cashier　：What's your room number please, madam?

Customer：Room 536.

Cashier　：Did you receive any billable service this morning, madam?

Customer：No, I didn't.

Cashier　：Just a moment, and I'll have your bill ready. Here's your bill, and that comes to NT$6000.

Customer：That's OK.

Cashier　：How would you like to pay?

Customer：Do you take American Express?

Cashier　：I'm very sorry but we don't accept American Express. Do you have another card, Visa or Master card?

Customer：I have a Visa card.

Cashier　：May I have your card, please?

Customer：Here you go.

Cashier　：Thank you. Please sign on the dotted line. Here's a pen.

Customer：Here you go.

Cashier　：Thank you. Here are your Visa slip and credit card. I hope you enjoyed your stay with us, madam.

II. The wrong bill 錯誤的帳單

A customer is checking out.

Customer：I'd like to check out.

Cashier　：What's your room number, madam?

Customer：Room 201.

Cashier　：Here's your bill. The amount is NT5600.

Customer：Excuse me, there's a mistake on my bill.

Cashier　：What's the problem, madam?

Customer：I was charged for dry-cleaning, but I didn't use the service during staying here. I think you get me the wrong bill.

Cashier　：Just a moment, please. I'll check it for you.

　　　　　(After a few moment)

Cashier　：Sorry, madam. You're right. We made a mistake for the dry-cleaning charge. We're sorry for the inconvenience.

Customer：That's all right.

Cashier　：Here's the new bill. And how would you like to pay?

Customer：By Visa, please.

Cashier　：May I have your credit card, please?

Customer：Here you are.

Cashier　：Please sign on the dotted line.

Customer：Here you go.

Cashier　：Here are your slip and credit card. I hope you enjoyed your stay with us, madam.

 單字考驗區

I. Look at the following flags and match the country and currency.

請寫出與國旗相對應的國家及貨幣。

Flag	Country	Currency

II. Crossword Puzzle

Please circle the words about paying bills.

There are ten words in the puzzle.

請找出十個與付款相關的單字，單字排列方式有垂直、水平以及斜對角。

T	W	V	X	I	M	C	R	Y	M
X	N	A	S	E	R	V	I	C	E
R	T	E	M	P	V	K	T	N	O
X	E	B	M	I	I	N	R	E	C
X	E	C	Y	E	U	T	H	R	H
R	P	A	E	O	T	E	A	R	A
H	S	A	C	I	O	A	X	U	R
P	V	S	B	T	P	B	T	C	G
L	I	V	W	A	H	T	A	S	E
D	K	J	L	V	Q	J	G	O	B

文化通

　　出國旅行，食、衣、住、行都要用到錢，即使預先訂好住宿與交通、預先付款，或參加旅行團，到了當地，購物時還是會需要用到錢。因此，事先瞭解當地的貨幣、匯兌、消費文化等，是必要的。例如，有些地區信用卡或旅行支票的使用不普遍，就需要多帶一些現金；有些國家在機場兌換當地貨幣的匯率比市區銀行好。事先做好功課，可以省錢，又可以避免一些不必要的困擾。

　　因為文化差異，各地的消費習慣往往也不太一樣，如在台灣、中國大陸、東南亞一些國家購物，會要求折扣、殺價的情形，若將這樣的購物習慣帶到某些國家，可能就行不通，甚至是不禮貌的。如筆者在德國萊茵河畔一個小鎮，看上一個價格不低的咕咕鐘，詢問是否有折扣，結果，老先生板起臉來說，請到別家買！當時，真是覺得尷尬極了！問了當地人才知道，殺價行為會讓店家覺得是在質疑他們的訂價過高。接著2個星期的行程，特意觀察留意，果然，德國的店家是不二價的。

旅遊常用貨幣符號及代碼

貨幣名稱	符號	代碼	貨幣名稱	符號	代碼
新台幣	NT$	TWD	日圓	¥	JPY
美金	US$	USD	韓元	₩	KRW
歐元	€	EUR	泰銖	฿	THB
英鎊	£	GBP	新加坡元	S$	SGD
澳幣	A$	AUD	越南盾	₫	VND
人民幣	RMB ¥	CNY	港幣	HK$	HKD

Notes

Answer Key

Unit 1 Hotel Staff & Hotel Types

I.
1. valet
2. operator
3. porter
4. waitress
5. cashier
6. butler
7. manager
8. doorman

II.
1. C   2. D   3. F   4. B   5. G
6. A   5. E

III.
1. housekeeper
2. valet
3. porter
4. front desk clerk

Unit 2 Taking Reservations

I.

6. sixth	19. nineteenth
7. seventh	20. twentieth
8. eighth	21. twenty-first
9. ninth	22. twenty-second
10. tenth	23. twenty-third
11. eleventh	24. twenty-fourth
12. twelfth	25. twenty-fifth
13. thirteenth	26. twenty-sixth
14. fourteenth	27. twenty-seventh
15. fifteenth	28. twenty-eighth
16. sixteenth	29. twenty-ninth
17. seventeenth	30. thirtieth
18. eighteenth	31. thirty-first

II.

1. expiration	5. credit card
2. guest	6. booking
3. deposit	7. address
4. reservation	8. check out

The Ocean Cloud Hotel Reservation Form			
Guest Name：	Larry Robertson		
Address：	1336 University Boulevard, Taipei, R.O.C.		
Phone：	(886) 2 332-1780		
Room Type：	☐ Single	☑ Double	☐ Family
Date of Arrival：	June 10th		
Date of Departure：	June 13th		
Credit Card Number：	4563 3345 2578 9901		
Expiration Date：	12/19		

Unit 3 Checking in

I.

1. 姓
2. 名
3. 城市
4. 州
5. 國家
6. 郵遞區號
7. 國籍
8. 入住日期

9. 退房日期
10. 停留時間
11. 信用卡類別
12. 信用卡號碼
13. 有效期限
14. 持卡人姓名
15. 簽名

II.

```
+  +  +  +  +  +  +  +  +  +  +  R  +  E  +
+  Y  +  +  +  +  +  +  +  E  +  +  R  +
+  +  T  +  P  +  +  +  G  +  +  +  U  B
R  N  O  I  T  A  M  R  I  F  N  O  C  T  A
E  +  +  +  L  +  S  S  Y  E  +  +  +  A  G
T  +  +  +  +  A  T  S  R  C  +  +  +  N  G
N  +  +  +  +  R  N  U  P  +  N  +  +  G  A
U  +  +  +  A  +  T  O  V  O  +  A  +  I  G
O  +  +  T  +  R  +  O  I  +  R  +  C  S  E
C  +  I  +  A  +  U  +  +  T  +  T  +  A  +
+  O  +  P  +  C  +  +  +  +  A  +  +  +  V
N  +  E  +  H  +  +  +  +  +  +  N  +  +  +
+  D  +  E  L  A  V  I  R  R  A  +  +  +  +
+  +  R  +  +  G  U  A  R  A  N  T  E  E  +
+  +  +  +  +  +  +  +  +  +  +  +  +  +  +
```

Unit 4 Services & Facilities

I.
1. currency exchange service
2. tour desk
3. gym
4. laundry service
5. reception
6. banquet hall

II.
1. reception
2. lounge
3. conference
4. restaurant
5. café
6. sauna
7. gymnasium
8. steam room
9. gift shop
10. banquet hall

Unit 5 Room Types & Room Facilities

I.

1. mirror
2. wash basin
3. bathtub

4. shower nuzzle
5. hair dryer
6. bidet

II.

heater
remote control
telephone
mini bar
electric kettle
dresser
closet
hairdryer
razor
bathtub
Jacuzzi
wash basin
mirror
bidet
Facility

Unit 6 Directions & Symbols/ Signs

I.

1. exit

2. toilet

3. sign

4. elevator

5. lift

6. disturb

7. emergency

8. evacuation

II.

1. exit

2. fire extinguisher

3. floor plan

4. Please make up the room now.

5. Please do not disturb.

6. men's room

III.

1. fire extinguisher

2. emergency evacuation plan

3. Please make up the room now.

4. car park

5. Please do not disturb.

Unit 7 Housekeeping

I.
1. hanger
2. pillow
3. bath towel
4. band aids
5. toilet paper
6. razor
7. facial tissues
8. slippers
9. scrubber

II.
1. slippers
2. ashtray
3. shampoo
4. dental floss
5. slippers
6. band aids
7. comb
8. saucer

Unit 8 Restaurant & Bar

I.
1. Continental breakfast
2. Coffee
3. American breakfast
4. Jam
5. Scrambled
6. Cereals

II.
1. American style breakfast
2. butter
3. hash browns
4. Scrambled eggs

Unit 9 Complaints, Problems & Requests

I.
1. C   2. D   3. A   4. E
5. B   6. F

II.
1. I'll have someone to bring you a new one.
2. I'll send a repairperson to replace it.
3. I'll send a plumber to fix it right away.
4. I'll contact the Bell Desk immediately.
5. We can change you to another room.
6. I'll send somebody from maintenance to help you.

III.
1. smell of smoke
2. filthy
3. keeps dripping
4. noisy
5. refilled
6. not working

Unit 10 Complaints, Problems & Requests

I.

Flag	Country	Currency
	Taiwan	New Taiwan Dollar
	Japan	Japanese Yen
	British	British Pound
	America	US Dollar
	South Korea	Korean Won

II.

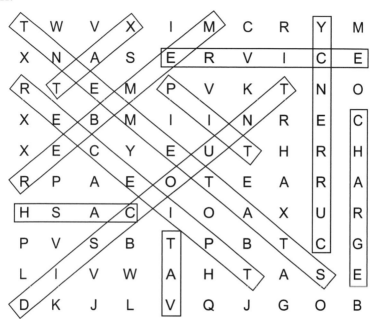

T	W	V	X	I	M	C	R	Y	M
X	N	A	S	E	R	V	I	C	E
R	T	E	M	P	V	K	T	N	O
X	E	B	M	I	I	N	R	E	C
X	E	C	Y	E	U	T	H	R	H
R	P	A	E	O	T	E	A	R	A
H	S	A	C	I	O	A	X	U	R
P	V	S	B	T	P	B	T	C	G
L	I	V	W	A	H	T	A	S	E
D	K	J	L	V	Q	J	G	O	B

單字	頁碼	中文
bathrobe	127, 136	浴袍，浴衣
bathtub	092, 164, 195	浴缸
bell captain	008, 018, 019	行李員領班
bidet	092, 164, 195	免治馬桶
bill (check)	004, 080, 173, 175, 177, 179, 180, 181, 182, 183, 184, 185, 187, 189 (177, 182, 183)	帳單
blanket	096, 126, 136	毯子
body lotion	129	乳液
boiled egg	144, 151	水煮蛋
brandy	147	白蘭地
breakfast included	028, 031, 034, 038, 040	含早餐
breakfast voucher	055, 057, 060	早餐券
buffet	037, 142, 148	自助式
bun	143	餐包
business center	069, 075	商務中心
business center attendant	011	商務中心服務員
business suite (executive suite)	087	商務套房
butler	012, 015, 191	私人管家
butter	143, 150, 152, 154, 155, 198	奶油
cable or satellite TV	089, 097 (089)	衛星或有線電視
café	069, 154, 194	咖啡廳
cake	143	蛋糕
cancellation policy	033, 042	退訂規則
car park	072, 113, 116, 196	停車場
cash	174, 179, 182	現金
cashier	010, 019, 179, 180, 181, 182, 184, 185, 191	出納
casino	072,	睹場（卡西歐）

單字	頁碼	中文
cereal (cornflakes)	145, 154, 198 (150, 152, 153)	玉米片
check in	014, 018, 019, 020, 029, 033, 039, 042, 050, 058, 059, 062, 064	住房
check out	029, 032, 035, 037, 039, 041, 050, 057, 060, 116, 182, 184, 185, 192	退房
check-in counter (front desk)	050, 058, 059	櫃檯
cheese	143	起司
children	029, 034, 039	孩童
Chinese Renminbi	174	人民幣
city/ town	030, 039,	城市
closet	091, 096, 195	衣櫃
coaster	124, 136, 151	杯墊
cocktail	114, 146, 149, 151	雞尾酒
coffee	124, 131, 145, 150, 153, 154, 198	咖啡
comb	128, 136, 197	梳子
concierge	008, 015, 018, 077, 078, 112,	櫃檯服務員
conference room	069	會議室
confirmation voucher	033, 037, 042, 052, 062	確認函
contact number	030, 034, 039, 043	連絡電話
cornice	123, 136	網狀毛刷
Could I have three cans of Taiwan beer and two packs of potato chips?	163	可以給我三罐台灣啤酒和兩包洋芋片嗎？
country	021, 030, 039, 062, 186, 200	國家
county/ province/ state	039	郡／省／州

單字	頁碼	中文
Euro	175	歐元
event planner	011	活動企劃人員
exit	108, 196	緊急逃生口
expiration date (validity date/ expiry date)	031, 035, 036, 040, 043, 045, 062, 192	有效期限
extra bed	029, 039, 094	加床
face towel	127	擦臉的毛巾
facial tissues	125, 197	面紙
family room (quad room)	028, 038, 086	親子房／四人房
fee	033, 042	費用
fire extinguisher	108, 112, 116, 196	滅火器
first floor	060, 105, 114	1樓（美式）
first floor	060, 105, 114	2樓 （英式）
first name (given name)	030, 036, 039, 062	名
fitness center attendant	011	健身中心服務員
floor plan	104, 196	樓層圖
floor towel	127, 131	地板巾
fried egg	144, 148, 150, 151, 152	煎蛋
front desk clerk	008, 014, 017, 018, 019, 020, 043, 191	飯店前檯服務人員
fruit	145, 150, 154	水果
gender	054	性別
gift shop	070, 111, 194	禮品店
gin	147, 149	琴酒
go along	107, 113	沿著…走
go straight	107, 113	直走
ground floor	105,	1樓（英式）
guest (occupant)	013, 014, 017, 018, 019, 020, 029, 030, 034, 039, 043, 045, 056, 057, 059, 060, 061, 095, 096, 097, 111, 112, 114, 124, 133, 134, 152, 153, 155, 164, 165, 192 (029, 039)	房客姓名

單字	頁碼	中文
guest name	030, 039, 045, 192	房客姓名
gym/ gymnasium	070, 075, 078, 081, 194	健身房
hair conditioner	129	潤髮乳
hairdryer	092, 165, 195	吹風機
ham	144, 154	火腿
hand towel	127, 134, 136	擦手巾
hanger	125, 197	衣架
hash browns	145, 148, 155, 198	薯餅
heater	089, 195	暖器
honeymoon suite	087	蜜月套房
Hong Kong Dollar	174	港幣
hostel (youth hostel)	006, 013, 021	青年旅舍
hotel	0101	旅館，飯店
hotel manager	008	飯店經理
hotel room sign (hotel room signage)	108	房間指示標示
housekeeper	010, 015, 016, 019, 020, 132, 133, 134, 164, 191	房務員
housekeeping cart	123	清潔推車
ice cube	146	冰塊
ID (identification)	053, 056	證件
I'm still waiting for my luggage.	163	我還在等我的行李。
in front of	107	在…前面
inn	007, 014, 021	小旅館
internet access	071, 075, 081, 090, 097	網路設施
invoice	178, 180	發票
iron & ironing board	091	熨斗及熨衣板
Jacuzzi	092, 097, 195	按摩浴缸
jam	143, 150, 154, 198	果醬
Japanese Yen	175, 200	日幣
JCB	176	JCB卡

單字	頁碼	中文
no show	033, 042	未出現
No. of nights (length of stay)	029, 039, 054, 058, 062	停留時間
non-smoking	029, 039	非吸煙的
omelet	144, 151	蛋餅，蛋捲
on the left/ on the left-hand side	107, 113, 114	在左手邊
on the right/ on the right-hand side	107, 111, 114	在右手邊
on-line booking	028, 034	線上訂房
operator	009, 191	接線生
passport	053, 056, 059, 063	護照
pay-per-view movies	090	按次付費電影
pillow	126, 131, 136, 197	枕頭
Please do not disturb.	110, 112, 116, 196	請勿打擾
Please make up the room now.	110, 112, 116, 196	請整理房間
polishing machine	123	磨光機
porter (bell boy/ bellhop/ bell person/ busboy)	009, 014, 020, 057, 060, 191	行李員
presidential suite	087	總統套房
Q tips (cotton swab)	128	棉花棒
quilt	096, 126, 131, 136	被子
razor	092, 129, 195, 197	刮鬍刀
receipt	177, 179	收據
reception	068, 075, 080, 081, 114, 194	接待櫃檯
receptionist	011, 114	接待員
registration form (check-in form)	051, 056, 059, 062	住房登記表
remote control	089, 195	搖控器
resort	007, 013, 021	渡假飯店

單字	頁碼	中文
restaurant	004, 016, 019, 060, 068, 114, 141, 148, 152, 153, 194, 198	餐廳
room card/ room key	055, 060	房卡／房間鑰匙
room division manager	010	房務部經理
room number	054, 056, 060, 108, 184, 185	房號
room number sign	108	房間號碼
room rate	028, 034, 038	房價
room service	078, 166, 167	客房服務
room type	004, 028, 038, 045, 085, 086, 192, 195	房型
room with a balcony	028, 038, 088	陽台房（有陽台的房間）
room with a view	088,	景觀房
rum	147	蘭姆酒
safe deposit box (safety box)	090, 094, 096, 097	保險箱
salad bar	142	沙拉吧
saucer	124, 136, 197	杯碟
sauna	071, 194	三溫暖
sausage	143, 150, 153, 155	香腸
scrambled egg	144, 148, 151, 152, 154, 155, 198	炒蛋
scrubber	122, 136, 197	刷子，擦布
second floor	105, 114	2樓（美式）
service charge	178, 179	服務費
sewing kit	125	針線包
shampoo	129, 132, 136 197	洗髮精
sheet	126, 131, 133, 136, 166, 168	床單
shower cap	128, 136	浴帽
shower gel (body shampoo, bath gel)	138, 132, 136	沐浴精

單字	頁碼	中文
shower nozzle	093, 096	蓮蓬頭
shuttle bus	074, 076	接駁車
signature	054, 062, 063	簽名
single room	028, 038, 045, 056, 086, 095, 101, 192	單人房
slippers	125, 136, 197	拖鞋
smoking	029, 039	吸煙的
soap	128	香皂
SPA	013, 021, 070	水療館
special requirements/ additional requests	029, 032, 035, 041, 057	額外要求
spot remover	123	去汙劑
squeegee	122, 130, 136	橡皮刮板
standard room	087	標準房型
statement (bill breakdown)	177, 183	帳單明細
steam room	071, 194	蒸氣浴房
stripper	122, 136	強效清潔劑
suite	021, 086, 087, 097	套房
sunny-side up	144, 148, 150, 152	太陽蛋
superior room	088	高級客房
surcharge	033, 042	額外費用
swimming pool	071, 081	游泳池
take the lift	075, 106, 111	搭電梯
take the lift to the 3rd floor	106, 111	搭電梯到3樓
tax	028, 030, 038, 178, 180	稅
tea	124, 133, 146, 150, 154, 157	茶
tea bag; coffee bag	124	茶包；咖啡包
teaspoon	124, 136	湯匙
telephone	062, 081, 090, 195	電話
tequila	147	龍舌蘭酒

釀語言8　PD0019

 圖解旅館英文詞彙

作　　者	張雅端、吳玉珍、柳瑜佳、張素蓁
責任編輯	廖妘甄
圖文排版	賴英珍
封面設計	秦禎翊

出版策劃	釀出版
製作發行	秀威資訊科技股份有限公司
	114 台北市內湖區瑞光路76巷65號1樓
	電話：+886-2-2796-3638　傳真：+886-2-2796-1377
	服務信箱：service@showwe.com.tw
	http://www.showwe.com.tw
郵政劃撥	19563868　戶名：秀威資訊科技股份有限公司
展售門市	國家書店【松江門市】
	104 台北市中山區松江路209號1樓
	電話：+886-2-2518-0207　傳真：+886-2-2518-0778
網路訂購	秀威網路書店：http://www.bodbooks.com.tw
	國家網路書店：http://www.govbooks.com.tw
法律顧問	毛國樑　律師
總 經 銷	創智文化有限公司
	236 新北市土城區忠承路89號6樓
	電話：+886-2-2268-3489　傳真：+886-2-2269-6560
	博訊書網：http://www.booknews.com.tw

| 出版日期 | 2013年9月　BOD一版 |
| 定　　價 | 400元 |

國家圖書館出版品預行編目

圖解旅館英文詞彙 / 張雅端等合著. -- 一版. -- 臺北市：
釀出版, 2013.09
　　面；　公分. -- (釀語言8 ; PD0019)
BOD版
ISBN 978-986-5871-71-0(平裝)

1. 英語　2. 旅館業　3. 詞彙

805.12　　　　　　　　　　　　　　　102013050

讀 者 回 函 卡

感謝您購買本書，為提升服務品質，請填妥以下資料，將讀者回函卡直接寄回或傳真本公司，收到您的寶貴意見後，我們會收藏記錄及檢討，謝謝！如您需要了解本公司最新出版書目、購書優惠或企劃活動，歡迎您上網查詢或下載相關資料：http:// www.showwe.com.tw

您購買的書名：_____

出生日期：_____年_____月_____日

學歷：□高中 (含) 以下　　□大專　　□研究所 (含) 以上

職業：□製造業　□金融業　□資訊業　□軍警　□傳播業　□自由業
　　　□服務業　□公務員　□教職　　□學生　□家管　□其它_____

購書地點：□網路書店　□實體書店　□書展　□郵購　□贈閱　□其他

您從何得知本書的消息？

　□網路書店　□實體書店　□網路搜尋　□電子報　□書訊　□雜誌

　□傳播媒體　□親友推薦　□網站推薦　□部落格　□其他_____

您對本書的評價：（請填代號　1.非常滿意　2.滿意　3.尚可　4.再改進）

　封面設計____　版面編排____　內容____　文／譯筆____　價格____

讀完書後您覺得：

□很有收穫　□有收穫　□收穫不多　□沒收穫

對我們的建議：_____

_____

_____

_____

11466
台北市內湖區瑞光路 76 巷 65 號 1 樓

秀威資訊科技股份有限公司　　　收

BOD 數位出版事業部

⋯⋯⋯⋯⋯⋯⋯⋯⋯⋯⋯⋯⋯⋯⋯⋯⋯⋯⋯⋯⋯⋯

（請沿線對折寄回，謝謝！）

姓　　名：＿＿＿＿＿＿＿＿　年齡：＿＿＿＿　性別：□女　□男

郵遞區號：□□□□□

地　　址：＿＿＿＿＿＿＿＿＿＿＿＿＿＿＿＿＿＿＿＿＿＿

聯絡電話：(日)＿＿＿＿＿＿＿＿＿　(夜)＿＿＿＿＿＿＿＿＿

E - m a i l：＿＿＿＿＿＿＿＿＿＿＿＿＿＿＿＿＿＿＿＿＿